GOOD BOOKS & BAD RIDDANCE

A Maximo Morgan Mystery

MARCH

WILLIAM LEROY

All rights reserved. Published by Mossik Press.

mossikpress@mail.com

Library of Congress Cataloguing-in-Publication Data

LeRoy, William [4.1.2025]

Good Books & Bad Riddance / Keeping It Real
by William LeRoy

p. cm
ISBN 979-8-9869494-9-9

1. Humor—Fiction.
2. Oklahoma, United States—Fiction.
3. Mystery—Fiction.
4. Noir—Fiction.
I. Title

10 9 8 7 6 5 4 3 2 1

Manufactured in the United States of America
First Edition

GOOD BOOKS & BAD RIDDANCE

A Maximo Morgan Mystery

MARCH

WILLIAM LEROY

TUESDAY

March 18, 2025

CHAPTER ONE

Max ankled into the Mister Quickie copy shop cubicle that served as his P.I. office and…

♫You've been sharpening your forks/ And poking at my cat… ♫

What the heck? Tanker Dan—"The Insecticidal Maniac"—was back already. Not whistling while he worked as usual.

♫You've been tasting our love letters/ And throwing up into my hat… ♫

Now the Good Riddance Company exterminator was softly singing words of the "Woodbox Gang" tune that usually blared from the tanker buggy he towed around town like a good humor man.

♫You've been hiding in our walls/ And plotting with a mouse… ♫ he sang, squirting poison here and there with a wand attached by hose to a tank strapped onto his back.

Yeah, Quickie's bright idea of putting a vending machine in the workstation cubicle might have baited a few snackers, but left-over muffin and cookie crumbs had also attracted an invasion of bugs.

♫You're always hungry… ♫

Plopped into his double-wide chair, Max watched with envy as the busy exterminator carried on with his work.

♫And want to eat our house… ♫

Not just his office but his entire hometown turf of Henryetta, Oklahoma, seemed to be crawling with vermin lately, except for the human variety that called for private dick squirting.

♫You've been making long-distance crawls/ From our bed to our telephone/ Watching us undress/ When we think we are alone… ♫

Yours Truly had not had a lay to work since handling *Case of An Unwatched Pot*, while the insecticidal maniac must have been busier than the proverbial one-armed paperhanger with a case of hives.

♫You"ve been sleeping with my wife/ When she's tucked in at night… ♫

With a sigh, Max took from a desk drawer a plaque identifying him by name as Maximo Morgan.

♫When you hear her sobbing/ You've been screaming: "Let the bed bugs bite!"♫

With another sigh, he retrieved another plaque identifying his game as…

"'Private Investigations'?" said Tanker Dan, taking off his red MAGA cap and raising the goggles he also always wore. "I thought you were a Notary Public."

"Yeah, Yours Truly stamps documents for copy shop customers as a sideline," Max explained, reaching into the drawer for his stamper. "Pays the cubicle rent between private dicking gigs."

"Hmmm," the good ridder hmmmed. "Except for the true one about Oprah's latest loss of 'lard', I'm not one to spread conspiracy theories, but…"

Max's ears perked up.

"Hmmm, I probably shouldn't tell you this, but…"

"Squirt it, Dan!"

After more hemming-and-hawing, the pint-size pest controller lowered his voice and told that in his professional opinion a recent outbreak of termite infestation was not the result of natural causes. In fact, the reluctant whistleblower continued, he had reason to suspect that the town's new haberdasher—"a foreigner, going by the name 'J. Markham'"—was smuggling an especially voracious sub-species of termites into the country.

"Hmmm," Max himself hmmmed.

"For crying out loud, Maximo, if the haberdasher's not

stopped the sneaky bastards will eat every building, every piece of wood, every sheet of paper in town. 'Good Riddance' is my motto, and I'm doing what I can to rid the town of the foreign menace. But Markham is technically not a termite and… We need a hero with the know-how and courage to put a kibosh on the plot to hollow-out our American way of life!"

On one hand, Max had a hunch the maniacal insect ridder's suspicions about a termite invasion and its source might amount to nothing but an unfounded personal conspiracy theory. On the other hand, Tanker Dan was in position to be in the know. And yeah, Oprah Winfrey's latest sudden weight loss could be explained as her delivery of another forty-pound Xi Jinping so-called "love child". So…

Max rose from his double-wide chair. He himself had private dick know-how, private dick courage, and had always wanted to be a hero. Inside his bean, he opened *Case of Foreign Infestation*.

CHAPTER TWO

♫If you're blue, and don't know where to go to/ Why don't you go where fashion sits… ♫

As sidewalk speakers broadcast a theme song of sorts to subtly lure passersby into his new store, Markham Joseph, Jr. a/k/a J. Markham dressed a Main Street show window to also subtly attract customers. He had been open for business only a few weeks and sales had been slow—almost non-existent actually—but as an apprentice of sorts to his late father over fifty years ago, he'd learned that it took time to educate hinterlanders about the value of high-quality haberdashery.

And after being away from the trade for over forty years, he was breaking new ground, both as a newcomer to town and trendsetter in upscale menswear.

♫Dressed up like a million-dollar trouper/ Trying hard to look like Gary Cooper… ♫

"Buy Yiddish and sell British" was his old man's motto. And while he himself—though well traveled—had never actually been to England, he had picked up a habit of drawling with a long-a, and adopted the name J. Markham Ltd. for his shoppe in the small town of Henryetta, Oklahoma. Sure, London's Saville Row or New York's 5th Avenue would have been a preferred venue for his re-entry into the rags biz, but…

♫Have you seen the well-to-do/ Up and down Park Avenue/ High hats and Arrow collars/ White spats and lots of dollars…♫

His current, considerably younger and relatively new spouse, Fidelita, had washed ashore on Key West, where he was, uh, in retirement at the time, and—based on matching progressive points of view—they had hit it off like Bogey and Bacall. It was Fidelita and her teenaged daughter, Chela, who had made him realize that working people—those who labored in overheated subterranean boiler rooms, for instance—were more deserving of decent clothes than fat cats sitting on their asses in air-conditioned penthouse board rooms.

♫Different types who wear a day coat/ Pants with stripes and cutaway coat/ Perfect fits for... ♫

Fidelita held the purse strings—having come to America with her life savings—and as a Venezuelan exile longed for the safety and security afforded, so to speak, in America's heartland. Coincidentally, the small town of Henryetta happened to be almost exactly halfway between Washington, D.C. and Los Angeles. So...

♫Why don't you go where fashion sits?... ♫

Though never a blue-collar type himself, he'd noted that while Duluth Trading Company now had a national chain of stores specializing in workwear—only a few years after coming out with its iconic Longtail T-Shirts designed to cover "plumber's cracks"—the chain's merchandizing was condescendingly down-market and popular-priced. So...

♫Puttin' on the Ritz... ♫

J. Markham finished off the show window by putting a bright red plastic carnation in a buttonhole of the outfit now displayed on a manikin... stepped back to admire his handiwork, and... Aha! On the sidewalk an overweight passerby, ridiculously dressed in an old-fashioned double-breasted suit—albeit tastefully decorated with a red plastic carnation in the buttonhole of a lapel—was eyeing the lure like a hungry big-mouth bass.

Out of the show window and onto the sales floor just as the customer jumped into his boat, so to speak...

"Looking for anything in particular, Mr.... ?"

"Maximo Morgan's the name. And as a matter of fact..."

"Shall we make it Maximo and plain J?"

"Yeah, Mahximo and Jah is okay if that's the way they say it overseas. What Yours Truly is looking for are..."

"Look no further than the herringbone outfit on display in the window. Wears like iron. Suitable for both boiler room big shots and board room—pardon the expression—fat cats."

"'Faht cahts'? You mean…?"

"I mean the choice is yours," said J. Markham, steering the customer to a rack of suits. "Woolens, worsteds, tweeds, flannels, mohair, moleskin. Blue, black or muted colors for business hours. Plaids, checks, houndsteeth for casual wear. And for today only…"

"Yeah, but as you can see, I'm a pinstriped kind of guy and…"

"Oh yes, stripes—vertical—for a slimming effect. And whereas a suit's 'drop'—the difference in chest-to-waist measurement—is usually on the order of minus-six inches, for pear-shaped gentlemen such as yourself I would not recommend double-breasted."

"Yeah, but you see…"

"I see you, Maximo, in one of these pleated Boston Whaler styles, with adjustable waist fasteners for plenty of breathing room. Notice the crotch—or what we call the 'fork'—where inseams come together. In a Whaler you can dress left or right, or let the 'hammer' hang right down the middle."

"Hahmmer?"

"There's a traditional loop sewn onto the right pantleg for the other one, heh, heh. Now, as for the 'seat' that covers your backside, I happen to have on hand an extra bolt of chalk-striped…"

"Sorry, Markham, but Yours Truly sports only double-breasted pinstripes, along with floral ties and a felt fedora like Brad Runyon a/k/a the Fat Man wore back in the *Noir*. Runyon was also overweight, but light on his feet and a good dancer, known as a natty dresser and …"

"The bibs provide a double-breasted effect, Maximo. You can wear neckties under the bibs for a vest-like look, or on the outside for a more casual look, except of course when you're working with machinery that has moving parts. And the patch pockets allow easy access to small tools and…"

"Save your breath, Markham. Yours Truly doesn't work with

moving parts and doesn't wear bib overalls made of worsteds, woolens, tweeds, mohair, moleskin or any cloth of any shape, size, pattern or color. I'm a private dick, looking into…"

Private detective? Looking into old debts?… old marriages?… prior run-ins with… ?

"… a sudden and suspicious local outbreak of termites," the fat man said.

J. Markham had a sudden outbreak of sweat. His wife cultivated termites to make a Venezuelan hot sauce called *kumachi*. There was nothing illegal or unhealthy about the condiment, but Fidelita and Chela had arrived in Key West by raft via Cuba without papers, and had not yet applied for political asylum.

"Let's check for what's hidden in these floorboards," said the fat man, before stomping a foot shod in hopelessly out-of-fashion brown-and-white wingtips.

Damnit, he had warned Fidelita they were likely to be confronted in the hinterland by heavy-handed—and heavy-footed—right-wingers. But the wife—as though on a mission—had been determined to nest in the small Oklahoma town, where the notion of "puttin' on the ritz'—J. Markham now realized—had more to do with putting cheese on crackers than dressing in fine workwear.

CHAPTER THREE

♫ *Termites ate my woody/ Termites ate my woody/ Termites ate my woody…* ♫

With the repetitive refrain of an old song from the distant past echoing inside his bean, Max ankled along Main Street, relieved to have the J. Markham workwear "shoppe" in his rearview mirror.

♫ *Termites ate my woody/ Termites ate my woody…* ♫

Markham, an odd duck, had admitted to having an "acquired taste" for termites that his Venezuelan Missus cooked up. So Yours Truly had cased the joint for the haberdasher's stash. No soap. At least, not enough "soap" to get lathered up about. Inside family quarters above the shoppe, yeah, a Spanish-speaking dame had copped to raising termites in a waterless aquarium of sorts. She willingly showed a couple of Mason jars containing wingless insects, and offered a sample of so-called *kumachi* on a cracker.

♫ *Termites ate my woody! Termites ate my woody!…* ♫

But the quarters were too cramped for large-scale bug ranching capable of producing an army of invaders. And just to make sure, Yours Truly had jumped up-and-down a few times — without detecting sagging floorboards such as termites were said to have a taste for — but stirring up personal nightmares about the terrifying threat posed by the wood eaters, invisible except as portrayed in Saturday morning tv shows for kids.

♫ *Termites ate my woody/ Termites ate my woody/ Termites ate my woody…* ♫

In a long ago Abby's Flying Fairy School segment of *Sesame Street*, for instance, the student named Blogg turned himself into a wooden puppet and started dancing right in front of a hungry termite. Luckily for Blogg, the wood eater ran away after taking a bite and complaining that it tasted like feet. But it had been a close call and…

♫ *Termites ate my woody!…* ♫

Earworms were what the silent musical echoes that afflicted him were called and, according to Dr. Gloria Stern — a shrink he had spent some time with at his mom's insistence — everyone had them from time to time. In his case, they supposedly represented suppressed thoughts and anxieties mainly resulting from a deep-seated "Edible Complex" going back to when he was a toddler in competition with his father for food. But post-toddling traumas could also trigger invasions by the little buggers and…. Come to think of it, the head-shrinker had quoted someone saying that ignoring the so-called subconscious was like neglecting termites in an attic.

♫ *Termites ate…* ♫

Arrived at the intersection of Main Street and 5th Street, Max put his gumshoeing in *Case of Foreign Infestation* on pause, wondering if Tanker Dan had given him a bum steer and debating with himself whether to turn back. But no, according to the expert exterminator, an invasion of termites threatened to eat every building, every piece of wood, and every sheet of paper in town. And moldy books would likely make a tempting dish for starters. With a sigh, he crossed Main Street.

Inside the one-story red brick public library building that once served as the town's post office — long before his twenty-five year stint of service in USPS uniform — he sniffed the air, but detected only the familiar sickeningly sweet odor of…

"Well, well, Maxwell Morgan," said Ms. Paroo, the town's longtime bookkeeper, parked at a desk littered with potted mini cactus plants. "Drawn like a busy bee by the aroma of my *Gay Paree* rose water, no doubt."

"Dropped by to peruse," said Max, not wanting to alarm the dowdy broad and risk triggering an onset of her ladylike vapors.

At shelves identified by sign as containing books about

CRIME/ MYSTERIES, he knew from past perusals he would not find pulp reports of cases handled by Mike Hammer, Phillip Marlowe, Sam Spade and other hardboiled dicks back in the *Noir*. Too lurid for the bookish library crowd, no doubt. Yeah, modern-day readers were squeamish about hardboiled back-alley tactics employed by Hammer, Marlowe, Spade and Yours Truly. But when trouble reared an ugly head, Jessica Fletcher? Fugetaboutit.

Instead, he randomly selected for inspection an old case report titled *Murder in the Rue Morgue*, a well known account of an amateur French sleuth's handling of a mysterious double-murrrderrr jotted by an Edgar Poe. He opened the paperback… detected no signs of termite damage… and randomly read:

"It will be found, in fact, that the ingenious are always fanciful, and the truly imaginative never otherwise than analytic."

Yeah, in what was said to be the first "modern detective story"—pre-dating Doc Watson's accounts of Sherlock Holmes' cases by almost fifty years—Poe described the amateur French P.I. named C. Auguste Dupin as a master of "ratiocination". Fancy foreign word for the doping-out technique Yours Truly would have used to detect that only a pet orangutang could have committed the grisly *Rue Morgue* crimes and escaped from a fourth-floor room found locked from the inside.

"How long are you going to be, Maxwell?" Ms. Paroo shouted from her stool. "It's almost lunch time and I'll have to lock up."

Max didn't bother to check any of a grouped row of familiar books… *The Choirboys… L.A. Confidential… Internal Affairs… Touch of Evil…* others about dirty cops and—in the case of *The Killer Within Me*—a murrrderrrous psychopathic lawman. Termites were welcome to all of them in his book. Yeah, he had a low opinion of flatfoots in general, and no use for local Barney Fifes in particular, but only because Badges tended to get in the way of complicated investigations. No way was Yours Truly a "Defund the Police" guy. No way was Maximo Morgan on the side of BLM hooligans and other street gangs.

"Five more minutes, Maxwell! The noxious vapors in here are

giving me a headache!"

Max was surprised to find a published report for *Case of Peddler on The Route*, dating back to days of *Noir* and crediting Percy Wilson—some said incorrectly—with solving a case in which owners of a bicycle factory were baffled by chronic declines in revenue. Suspicious that a certain employee in their accounting department was somehow embezzling funds, the factory big shots had their own security personnel keep an eye on the suspect at work. No soap until they finally brought in Wilson. Within days the savvy private dick doped out that the accountant arrived at the bicycle factory on foot every morning, carrying a brown bag lunch; left work at the end of every day with the brown paper sack folded under an arm, and rode home on a bicycle!

After thumbing through the write-up of Wilson's "ratiocination" of the clever inside job—and detecting that not a single page had been nibbled on—Max picked up a bound collection of mysteries solved by the overseas hawkshaw, Hercule Poirot. The familiar case of *The Adventures of Johnny Waverly* involved another, though not clever inside job—Poirot's own client had kidnapped his own grandson—but… Ha! On another page of another case report…

"Mind how you get on there, Poirot. This is wasp country. Nasty nest of them out by that old tree. I myself have been stung three times this summer."

"Oh no!… Oh!… Oh!… I have hatred for these crawling, buzzing things. And the reason is, they are trying to kill me!"

"I had Claude out here last week. But no dice. He's coming to have another go tonight."

Yeah, in *Case of The Wasps' Nest*, the prissy overseas P.I. got stung due to faulty riddance, and as Max vaguely recalled…

"Time's up, Maxwell," the antsy librarian shouted.

"Any signs of termites on the premises, Ms. Paroo?" he routinely asked on his way out of the stacks of moldy books.

"Are you kidding? If you ask me, the Library Board overdoes extermination. I've had to squirt gallons of *Eau de Seine* to cover up the odor."

Passing by a shelf labeled U.S. HISTORY/GOVERNMENT, however, Max detected what looked to be little piles of... Running a finger across the undusted edge of a shelf... he noticed on the floor what looked to be tiny dried-out wings of... He opened a book titled *The American Story: Building of a Republic* and... Bingo. The history had been hollowed out!

He opened another volume titled *Our Constitution: Protection Against Tyranny of a Majority,* and...

"All the pages have been eaten!"

"Well, don't look at me!" said chubby librarian, with a jerk of her head toward a wall-mounted sign: NO FOOD ALLOWED IN LIBRARY. "It must be those hopped-up teenagers who come in here with the 'munchies'."

Yeah, maybe, but... Though fearful of causing panic, Max stomped a foot... stomped again and...

"Stop it, you fool!" Ms. Paroo shouted...

... as he sank, terrified, through the library floor into the building's crawl space.

CHAPTER FOUR

♫Elephants and termites, one giant, one so small/ When elephants get itchy butts, they squirm and jump and twitch... ♫

Daphne Baldwin sat in a lawn chair outside her sod farmhouse, listening for a second time to a song by William Shatner a/k/a Captain Kirk.

♫It's not like they can use their trunks to scratch a nasty itch... ♫

Being both a "Trekkie" and longtime animal rights activist, she had splurged on the album of children's songs titled *Where Will the Animals Sleep* — and borrowed a grandchild's cd player — after reading that the beloved commander of the Starship Enterprise had joined the fight to save life on Planet Earth, but...

♫The termites build up piles of mud and dirt, into massive twelve-foot mounds/ The elephants will rub themselves against them to make the itches go away .. ♫

Disappointed and disgusted, Daphne turned off the cd. Yes, the song would go on to make a point of sorts: Once the termite mounds collapsed due to elephant scratching, the ground beneath would become a pool in which other species fed and bred. But she herself had progressed through the years into a particular sub-subset of the eco-animal rights movement.

In the mid-Nineties, moved by the *Free Willy* movie, she had joined violent protests demanding that the film's star — an adorable Orca named Keiko — be returned to the wild. After Keiko's release she had personally dumped whole buckets of tofu into his native Norwegian waters.

Devastated by the Hollywood star's premature death—possibly due to dietary issues—she had become a card-carrying member of the supposedly "radical" Animal Liberation Front. As an ALF warrior she had thrown numerous Molotov cocktails at various enemy facilities such as police stations, meat packing plants, university labs and restaurants. All to no avail. The voracious global capitalistic system had continued to slaughter five billion animals a day to feed human lust for meat. As famously noted by someone famous: if people in China were driven by capitalism and developed a taste for seafood equal to that of Japanese people, there would not be a fish in the ocean within a year.

Charged as a domestic terrorist 2005, she had retreated to the Baldwin family's Oklahoma farm, where for the past twenty-plus years she and her numerous children, together with their numerous spouses and children, had dug in for a last stand. In a circle of sod houses connected by tunnels, workers tended to the feeding. Soldiers protected the commune.

Some said they were "malcontents" and/or "doomsday preppers". True enough. Most in the surrounding backward area called them Communists. But they adhered to no ideology for advancement of human welfare. To the contrary, a song titled *Inside the Termite Mound* by a group called Killer Joke was their anthem, not the *Internationale*. Standing tall in the center of the compound, a large termite mound in fact served as a kind of totem around which the family often stood, chanting "Consume to Live! Live to Consume!", and singing…

♫*Antennae tuned to inhuman vibrations/ Shaping the cities of the world to come/ I listen to the sound, the endless construction/ Inside the termite mound…* ♫

Yes, the Baldwin family identified, secretly but proudly, with termites. And why not? Though beset by predators, including ants mainly, but also centipedes, cockroaches, crickets, dragonflies, spiders, reptiles, toads and mice—not to mention unspeakable human exterminators such as "Tanker Dan"—termites were the last hope for survival of life on Earth.

♫*Serving their purpose/ It's their purpose to serve/ A thousand lights from this honeycombed labyrinth. .* ♫

And Daphne, as the "queen", so to speak, had the responsibility to…

In the distance, a trail of dust signaled the return from school of her teenaged son, Billy. She had high hopes for her youngest offspring, but worried that he would go astray like her rebellious oldest. Like his big brother, Billy had developed a potentially dangerous interest in… Yes, now she could see that the high-spirited Venezuelan girl was riding on the back of his motorbike. Once upon a time, she herself had been…

"Yo, Mom, you remember Chela," Billy said after racing around the termite mound and coming to a stop at their sod doorstep.

"Nice to see you again, *Senora* Baldwin," said the dark-eyed girl.

"Chela was hoping we could spare a few more termites, Mom."

More termites? Daphne's maternal antennae bristled. Though a devout vegan herself, she didn't object to other people eating the insects. Indigenous people in Africa as well as South and Latin America enjoyed the delicacies that were high in protein. Nor did she mind the Venezuelan girl taking a few specimens, but… More termites for only a spicy condiment called *kumachi*?

"My mother dropped and broke all three Mason jars," said the girl, but…

With her antennae fully up, Daphne noted that two nights ago the teenaged couple had spooned for hours beside the mound and…

♫*Nocturnal notions (As we leave our cocoon/) A thousand lights from this honeycombed labyrinth/ These winding tunnels lead to my place of desire…* ♫

"Be careful not to disturb the queen," said Daphne, though suspicious of what Chela was up to. In fact, other termites—when outside the mound—were miraculously capable of reproducing.

She herself had once plotted to loose an invasion into cities and towns, but now she was older and wiser. Destruction of human civilization was inevitable in the long term, but in the meantime, a visible attack would invite better-armed exterminators to vengefully "scratch their itchy butts" on termite homes.

CHAPTER FIVE

""Phew!"

On hands-and-knees in the attic of the modest frame house he had lived in since birth, Max was relieved. Despite his mom's neglect of the space, his late father's stash of pulp case reports had not, so far, been gobbled up by termites.

As a teenager, he himself had devoured, so to speak, the lurid accounts of cases handled by famous private detectives back in the *Noir*. In particular, he had been inspired to someday walk in gumshoes by repetitively digesting, so to speak, the ending of Mike Hammer's *Case of I, The Jury*... as jotted by Mickey Spillane... garishly illustrated on the book's cover... and still known to Yours Truly by heart:

"No, Charlotte, I'm the jury now, and the judge, and I have a promise to keep. Beautiful as you are, as much as I almost loved you. I sentence you to death."

Her thumbs hooked in the fragile silk of her panties and pulled them down. She stepped out of them as delicately as one coming from a bathtub . . .

Yeah, the roar of Mike's "Old Junior" shook the room. Those loving arms of the fickle *femme fatale* would have reached a hidden rod nicely. A face waiting to be kissed would have been splattered when she blew Mike's head off if the hardboiled hawkshaw had not plugged her first.

In Yours Truly's book, termite consumption of such records from back in the days and murky nights of *Noir* would be worse than the hollowing out of American history at the library, but...

Climbing down a ladder, Max conceded that he really

couldn't blame his mom for not calling Tanker Dan to squirt the attic. Heck, according to Ms. Paroo, the "Insecticidal Maniac" had regularly double-dosed the front area of the public library where she, her cactus plants, and the books about U.S. History and the U.S. Constitution were kept, and where the library floor had nevertheless collapsed under the weight of Yours Truly. In other words, the Good Riddance Company treatments were not cutting the mustard. So just dumb luck that his old man's "library" had escaped termite attack, and that he himself had dodged a broken leg by landing on his backside at the library.

Now landed safely on foot in a sturdy hallway and… Hello, the teenaged kid who jotted case reports for him was parked at the kitchen table, digging into a slice of apple pie.

"Your Mom let me in, Mr. Max," the kid explained. "I dropped by to see if anything has gone down that needs to be written up."

The young wannabe P.I. was a protege of sorts, but still green as two gardeners' thumbs. Yeah, while the teenager had also mastered the pulp accounts and film documentaries of the dickwork of famous gumshoes back in the *Noir* and could talk the talk, he had a long way to go before walking the walk. Strictly for jotting purposes, Max put the kid wise to Tanker Dan's alert that an infestation of termites threatened every building, every piece of wood and every sheet of paper in town.

"Riddle this, Mr. Max: A termite walks into a bar and says what?"

Max, in no mood for riddling, drew a blank.

"Is the bar tender here?… Get it?"

Put wise that *Case of Foreign Infestation* might have an even unfunnier punchline…

"Well yeah, there's a Minecraft game called *Termites Take Over the Village*, and I suppose termites could be a menace to mankind in real time," said the know-nothing high school know-it-all. "According to our Biology teacher, Mr. Walker, there are a thousand pounds of termites for every human on earth, and they are the world's most prolific farters. Termites emit a hundred and fifty million tons of methane gas every year, which is a major contributor to climate change."

Max wasn't interested in weather. He worried about the attic stash of pulp, not to mention the attic floor, as the bookish kid went on to recap either the rules for a computer game or a Biology class lecture.

Termites were a "societal species", sometimes referred to as "superorganisms" due to the collective behaviors of individual members in self-governing colonies as large as three million in population, the kid recapped. Each nest had a single queen, capable of living up to fifty years and producing 50,000 eggs per annum. They never slept, but worked 24/7, building underground nests and connected tunnels inside mud mounds that could reach two-stories in height. Ants were their worst enemy and, under a caste system, half a colony of termites were blind "soldiers" that, if the nest was attacked, banged their heads together to communicate, sprayed acid at intruders, and…

"Well, like the song by Greg Gobel goes, said the kid: ♫'Twas upon a misty night/ No, we weren't looking for a fight/ We heard them marching through the fog/ Setting to invade our log… ♫

What, another song about termites? Another potential earworm afoot?

♫Ants tried attacking through our holes/ in our tunnels, on they flowed/ But this is what they did not know/ We are soldier termites… ♫

For crying out loud, had teenaged dance crazes gone from the wholesome Jitterbug dating back beyond his mom's time to a 'Termite Hop'?

♫We're soldier termites, we explode! ♫

"See, Mr. Max, termite soldiers blow themselves up in tunnels sorta like suicide bombers, so nests are hard to get at by ants. Only well armed exterminators…"

"Yeah, very interesting, but Yours Truly has a hunch *Case of Foreign Infestation* will turn out to be along the lines of Poirot's *Case of The Wasps' Nest*, in which a careless exterminator didn't use strong enough juice and got sent back to town by Poirot's buddy for cyanide."

"Actually, Mr. Max, it was Mr. Poirot's friend himself who purposefully diluted the exterminator's juice, and sent him back to town for cyanide with intent to commit murrrderrr."

Human homicide?

The kid went on to explain that Poirot's friend was doubly bitter that the exterminator in that case was involved in illicit hanky-panky with his fiancee, and that he himself was about to kick a bucket.

"Aha, so Poirot's pal was himself a 'wasp', and turned tables by squirting the cyanide on the exterminator in a classic case of bait-and-switch!"

"No, Mr. Poirot's friend intended to poison himself, which would have framed the exterminator who had bought the cyanide, and result in the romantic rival being hanged."

Hmmm.

"Keep your eye on the ball, kid," said Max. "The 'switcheroo' this time is likely to be that dilution is the solution in a case of bad riddance."

"Maybe. But speaking of switcheroos, Mr. Max, it could be that our lay is more along the lines of the old Lucky Luke case—documented in an animated film—in which an evil mayor 'celebrated' completion of a wooden bridge into town by hitting the structure with a fake champagne bottle filled with termites, who ate the bridge before cavalry could cross it to rescue oppressed local citizens."

Occasionally the bookish kid came up with a lucky hunch, but... Nah, it would have been more than a hundred years ago that a local mayor might have smashed a champagne bottle against the public library building to celebrate the opening of what was then a post office. And in "our" case, there would have been evidence—likely eye-witness evidence— if the local haberdasher and his Venezuelan Missus had tossed a Mason jar filled with termites through a public library window. But the gabby kid...

"A new girl at school named Chela Castro is likely a Communist, Mr. Max."

Chela Castro? Step-daughter of J. Markham? A Communist?

"She brags about being named after Che Guevera, always wears tee-shirts with the Cuban terrorist's picture on it, and is Ms. Phlegming's new pet," the kid explained. "And she hangs with Billy Baldwin, who lives on a farm east of town, and knows more about termites than even our Biology teacher. Maybe we should quiz him, not Mr. Walker, but Billy Baldwin."

Baldwin? The name tinkled a bell, but... Though unable to come up with a match, Max decided that—before squirting industrial-strength dickwork on the Markham family nest of Commies—his next step in gumshoes would be to look up the young "termite expert".

WEDNESDAY

March 19, 2025

CHAPTER SIX

♫Terrible Terry the termite/ Crunch! Crunch! Crunch!/ Oh how he loves a free lunch… ♫

With another earworm doing its thing inside his head, Max drove his mom's brown Buick boiler into the countryside east of town. Dang it, it had taken years for him to "exterminate" the first ear pest that got to him— ♫It's a small world after all/ It's a small world after all/ It's a small world after all… ♫—while waiting in line for a Disney World ride. And years later, the wormy tune had come back with new words— ♫Duff beer for me/ Duff beer for you/ I'll have a Duff/ You have one too… ♫—in a Simpsons episode. Most recently, the pharmaceutical jingle— ♫I have diabetes, but I manage it well/ It's a little pill with a big story to tell♫—had been harder than baby poop imbedded in corduroy to get rid of.

And the usually recommended cure—forcing to mind another song—could be worse than the cure, as proven by his years of suffering to the tune of ♫Rump-titty-rump-titty-rump-rump-rump… ♫

♫He gnawed at the ceiling while Mom had her club/ And down came the bathroom with Pop in the tub/ Terrible Terry the termite/ Crunch! Crunch! Crunch!… ♫

At the local high school earlier, he himself had intended to get in the ear of a young Billy Baldwin, the teenager oddly and suspiciously said to be a termites expert and the boyfriend of the Markhams' daughter named Chela. But no soap. Neither Baldwin nor the girl had shown up for classes today. All he'd gotten out of a gang of juvenile delinquents hanging out behind the gym was that Billy was a "dirtball" and "dumb", Chela a "Commie" and "hot".

♫*I'm Terrible Terry the termite/ Crunch! Crunch! Crunch!/ (The one we'd like to punch!)…* ♫

Max recalled that as a post-toddler, sitting on the living room floor, watching Saturday morning cartoons and snacking, he—already overweight and pear-shaped but always hungry—had identified with Terry. But that was before he started having nightmares about the woody-eaters. And long before he had wised up to the fact of life that even teenaged *femmes*—such as Chela Markham—were capable of being *fatale*.

Heck, Eve was likely a teenager when she got Adam to eat that apple. Bonnie of Bonnie-and-Clyde notoriety and Laurie Stall in *Case of Gun Crazy* were young teens when they went on murrderrrous rampages. La Femme Nikita was a teenaged so-called "nihilist" committed to stirring up violent anarchy and destruction. And in Phillip Marlowe's *Case of the Big Sleep*, Carmen Sternwood—described as a "young, childish girl who likes to pull wings off flies"—famously tried to sit on the hardboiled dick's lap while he was standing up!

In other words, a "hot Commie" such as the Castro *femme* would have a "dumb dirtball" such as Billy Baldwin for lunch, so to speak.

♫*There was a barmaid I took down a peg/ I sneaked up behind her and ate her wooden leg/ Terrible Terry the termite/ Crunch! Crunch! Crunch!…* ♫

At a posted mailbox signed *Baldwin*, Max ignored a No Trespassing warning and steered the boiler onto a rutted dirt road. The farm was oddly treeless, he noticed as he drove toward a cluster of mounds in the distance and faintly heard…

♫I've been dancing in your shadow/ All over your bug light/ Singing in your sprinkler/ Building up an appetite… ♫

Yeah, another song was playing, not inside his bean, but on some kind of sound system.

♫Some houses are made of stone/ While some are made of

brick/ When I get through with yours… ♫

Arrived at the edge of a large cluster of what looked to be sod houses circled around a large mound of also dried mud… Max cut his ride's engine… got out of the boiler… and ankled toward the front stoop of a dirt house where a broad sat, rocking back and forth in a lawn chair and singing along with a recording.

♫I've been hiding in your walls/ And plotting with your mouse/ I am hungry/ And I'm gonna eat your house♫

"Whatta you want?" she hollered after turning off what looked to be a cd player in her lap. "Didn't you see the sign!"

"Maximo Morgan's the name. Private dicking is my game. And I'm looking to hear a little chin music from a certain Baldwin boy reputed to be a termite expert."

"What's he done this time?"

"Cut school for one thing, but what Yours Truly wants to hear about is…"

"Danny's gone back to school? Ha!"

Danny? OMG. The Baldwin name now rang a bell loud and clear.

"That snooty hairdresser he ran off with must have got him to put on bookish airs."

"Tanker Dan is your, uh, boy?"

"Not anymore," the odd broad snorted. "Not since he sold out to the capitalistic system, turned against the family with a vengeance, and became a damned 'insecticidal maniac'! We are termite sympathizers, and Danny is a termite killer."

"Hmmm," Max hmmmed, as the first recorded family feud—and first recorded case of murrrderrr—came to mind:

Two brothers, one a parental pet, the other not so much. In Yours Truly's case, one a termite sympathizer, the other a termite exterminator. Yeah, a switcheroo in *Case of Foreign Infestation* indicating a plot by Billy Baldwin a/k/a "Abel" against his brother, Dan a/k/a "Cain" to win their mom's approval… by diluting the insecticidal maniac's squirt juice… and putting local mankind in danger of falling through riddled floorboards!

CHAPTER SEVEN

♫ *There's no safe words/ There's no stasis/ There's no fixing the broken places...* ♫

Following an imagined standard intro comprised of a heavy metal cacophony of drums, electric guitars and snippet of a no doubt unintentionally "ironic" song—*End the Fight Before the Fight Ends You* by a group called Hatebreed—Peg Patterson mentally rehearsed an opening to today's *In the Arena* segment of WOKC-TV's *News at High Noon*:

Citizens of the small town of Henryetta, only ninety miles east of Oklahoma City, are at odds with one another on issues arising from an infestation of termites. In one corner...

Yes, termites! Without a camera crew in tow, she was driving her own car to a small, backwater town to report on a petty squabble over how to handle common household pests!

Peg sighed. Once upon a time—as host of *On the Spot With Peg Patterson*—she'd been the toothy smiling face of WOKC-TV, almost equal in celebrity to the station's weatherman, "Jumping Jack Flash" Ireland. Viewers throughout the State of Oklahoma had followed her daily changes of snappy outfits and breathless reports of important news stories almost as avidly as they quaked in excited fear during Jumping Jack's tornado warnings. But...

Peg again sighed. She'd given up fame and fortune to selflessly answer a call to public service. And shoulda, coulda, woulda been elected to the State Senate—with bright prospects for higher office—if not for circumstances surrounding the untimely death her husband, Gabe. For crying out loud, her selfish late spouse, a State Bureau of Investigation official, had tried to advance his own career by playing footsie with a Mexican drug lord. And she herself had been publicly suspected of running him off a road. Only after S.B.I. big shots covered up their own involvement in lethal office politics… and her lawyer filed a lawsuit… and she humiliated herself by again getting down on her knees like a needy newbie newsie…

♫Rump-titty-trump-titty-rump-rump-rump…. ♫

The call was from her boss, a young up-and-comer, not even the real WOKC-TV News Director. She put her phone on speaker and…

"Where are you, Peg? We're ten minutes from face-off," said the WOKC-TV Sports Director.

"I'm five minutes from ringside," Peg reported, as she exited the Interstate into the small town of Henryetta, proudly identified by water tower signage as "Home of Troy Aikman and Gaylord Goodheart", both former Dallas Cowboy quarterbacks.

"X, Tik Tok and Meta are cranking out rumors that an undercover F.B.I. agent warned the town librarian about a foreign plot to infest American history books with termites, and blamed a sudden collapse of a library floor on an attempt by foreign assassins to stop his investigation into a full-scale termite invasion. Get off ringside and into the arena, Peg."

As both a veteran news reporter, and former high school cheerleader, Peg didn't need to be told that conflict was the essence of every story of any interest, whether told on tv news or in novels, movies and sports broadcasts. Television companies had to pay to show, say, staged World Wrestling Entertainment contests between costumed agents of good versus agents of evil. Publishers, Hollywood movie makers and fight promoters had to pay writers and actors. But "reality" politics was free. And there was a potentially contentious political angle to virtually everything these days.

Invasion of termites, however… ugh, fundamentally borrrring in the extreme. It would take inspired journalism on her part to find an angle that captured viewers' attention, ginned up anger, and… And damnit, she didn't have the benefit of a WOKC-TV

News van and camera crew to draw concerned citizens into the arena like moths to a flame.

But this was not her first fish fry, Peg reminded herself as she parked her car on Main Street, a block from where a gaggle of gawkers had gathered. As a high school cheerleader she had ginned up parents to get involved in their boys' wholesome extra-curricular activities, by shouting: "Fight! Fight! Fight! Fight! Fight! / Hold that banner nice 'n' upright!/ Crowd the line and fight! fight! fight!/ Plunge it through 'er and do it twice!"

Now, as a news reporter—contrary to right wing charges of media bias in favor of, say, "saving democracy"—her job was to incite both sides of domestic conflict and fire up…

"This just in, Peg," said the Sports News Director through the phone. "In an unprecedented mid-day Breaking News appearance on MSNBC, Rachel Maddow brought on a former C.I.A. Director to confirm that our termite attack has all the markings of a Putin 'false flag' operation aimed at blaming progressives for gobbling the library book containing the U.S. Constitution. So be sure to provide context: say, little buggers selectively munching on the moldy document to take out our sacred right to report news, but leave intact the First Amendment right of uninformed dummies to engage in hateful free speech.

"And get this: Rachel reports that a bible, yes the Bible, was seen on the public library premises by an outraged citizen, undamaged! So it's a target-rich environment, Peg. Take no prisoners!"

Delighted that a possibly not so minor small town kerfuffle had caught the attention of national media, Peg got out of her car and hurried toward the cluster of people gathered outside a one-story red brick building, though only one concerned citizen was holding a protest placard on a stick.

Disappointed by not only the crowd's size, but also its lack of spirit—not to mention finding that the sign protested only library late return fees—she nevertheless sidled up to an angry-looking old man… held out her phone for a videoed selfie… put on her trademark toothy smile, and… cued by a musical blast from the WOKC-TV studio…

♫Forgetting nothing, forgiving so much less/ The devil you thought you never knew/ Is now the one that knows you best… ♫

"Peg Patterson, reporting live from *In the Arena* of the small, vulnerable American town of Henryetta. Tell me, Mister, are ready to fight, fight, fight the invasion of Russian termites?"

"Russian termites? Well, I'll be damned," he said, taking off a red MAGA cap to scratch his head. "On the other hand, we had an invasion of illegal Mexican killer bees a few years back, and they did a lot of strange buzzing between theirselves that must have been Spanish."

"Did you say Russian termites?!" said a chubby middle-aged woman, edging into the selfie. "Well, I'm damn sure ready to fight 'em off. Did you hear about the rapin' that Putin's soldiers did over there in… in… Thelma! Come over here and get your picture on tv!" she hollered. "The Russians are coming!"

The Russians are coming! others chanted…

The Russians are coming!

… and like wildfire…

The Russians are coming!

The Russians are coming!

The Russians are coming!

Curious if not yet concerned citizens poured out of stores and offices. Others parked cars and trucks—some right in the middle of Main Street—and came running on foot to see what was going on.

Call the National Guard!

Call the National Guard!

Call the National Guard!

A ginned-up citizen—also wearing a MAGA cap and conveniently armed with a bullhorn—jumped onto the hood of his car and shouted:

"Call the Bugbuster!"

"Yeah, call Tanker Dan!" the chubby middle-aged woman yelled.

"Are you crazy?" said a teenaged boy. "He's an insecticidal maniac!"

"Captain Kill will rid the town of every living creature!" said a dark-skinned girl, holding up a machine-printed FREE TERRY! placard. "It's a capitalist plot against worker termites, worker bees and worker people!"

"Termites are vital to the world's ecology" another youngish female shouted. "They are decomposers that rid the world of debris and enrich the soil."

"Yeah, and 'enrich' the air with gassy farts that make the weather hot!" another concerned citizen hollered in rebuttal.

Russians are coming!
Call the National Guard!
Call the Bugbuster!
Tanker Dan is a Maniac!

As curses, fists and feet began to fly—mainly, but not exclusively in contests between young and old—Peg continued to hold up her phone to film the action, while mentally composing a sign-off. Her onsite reporting would get her *In the Arena* segment on both MSNBC and Fox News, she was thinking, but…

"It's a wrap," the WOKC-TV Sports News Director informed her through an earbud. "Segue to commercial."

♫End the fight? Before the fight ends you/ Of all the lies I've told you/ This is the least untrue♫

CHAPTER EIGHT

Back at his desk, Max picked up his phone and—with both thumbs—started connecting dots backward: from mother of the teenaged termite expert, Billy Baldwin… to the Markham family of foreigners… to…

"Good Riddance," said a dame's voice. "Dottie speaking."

"Maximo Morgan on the blower," said Max. "Need to dot a i and cross a t with your top ridder."

"Dan's out on a job at the moment, but if you would care to leave a…"

"Dottie! Ms. Johnson's hair is smoldering!" a broad in the background of likely a beauty parlor bellowed.

With his own hair about to catch fire, so to speak, Max cooled his heels, so to speak. If Billy Baldwin and his Commie girlfriend were diluting Tanker Dan's extermination juice, the whole town could be…

"Good Riddance, Dottie speaking," said the likely Missus Baldwin, dissed by her mother-in-law as a snooty hairdresser.

Word of the library floor collapse had spread, she said. In panic, people were barraging the extermination company with urgent pleas for a squirt. Yeah, time—as private dicks dating back to Sherlock Holmes to Mike Hammer to Yours Truly often said—was of the essence.

Five minutes later, put wise by the harried hairdoer that her husband was working a big job at the Red Queen Company's cardboard box warehouse, Max put pedal to the metal of the brown boiler and drove toward what was left of the town's hollowed-out industrial area.

Once upon a time his hometown had twenty-three industrial plants, all owned by big out-of-town corporations. The largest Pittsburgh Plate Glass factory west of the Mississippi that employed nine hundred workers. And an Eagle-Picher smelting operation—now a so-called Superfund brownfields site—that produced three quarters of the free-world's supply of a rare metal called germanium. Population was about eight thousand, and the town was reported to be prosperous. Mom remembered there were two movie theaters for people to go to for wholesome entertainment, lots of stores, and plenty of jobs.

Those were Henryetta, Oklahoma heydays. Now the town's population was down to less than six thousand. Good jobs were scarce as good church goers. Now the so-called industrial area was dotted with a few small workshops, and mainly used for storage of one thing or another. Yeah, the hey was long gone.

Arrived at a chainlink-fenced parking lot signed *Employees Only,* Max got out of the boiler… pushed open a rusted metal gate… and hotfooted past a few old jalopies toward a large, red-brick building. Inside…

♫*La cucaracha, la cucaracha/ ya no puede caminar…* ♫ blasted from somewhere.

Without being asked for whereabouts of a man in charge, a janitor leaning on a broom pointed a finger in the direction of a big-bellied big shot standing in a shallow pool of water, holding a clipboard in one hand and a coffee mug in the other.

♫*Porque le falta/ porque no tiene…* ♫

After slamming a hammy fist against a nearby boom box to stop the music, the warehouse foreman—identified by nameplate as a Kowolski—apologized for the racket. "Keeps da workers movin'," he explained in possibly a Brooklyn or New Jersey accent straight out of the *On the Waterfront* documentary from back in the *Noir* about greedy corporations and corrupt labor unions exploiting dockworkers. "Drives me nuts."

Max likewise.

Giving the joint a once-over—eyeballing a few dark-skinned workers scurrying here and there like ants, or maybe cockroaches—he sensed that another annoying earworm from back in his early school days had infested his bean. Sure enough…

♫ *The cockroach, the cockroach/ Can't walk anymore/ Because he's missing/ Because he's missing/ Two little back legs/ La cucaracha, la cucaracha…* ♫

Otherwise, all he detected in the large warehouse space were high stacks of flattened sheets of cardboard and wood pallets.

"Dropped by to have a little chat with Tanker Dan, the Good Riddance Company exterminator," said Max.

"Sent 'im home," the burly boss man growled. "Been chargin' an arm-an'-leg for bad riddance. 'Waste Kills Profits' is a Red Queen Company motto an'… You's some kinda government inspector or somethin'? Hell, we've had more bugs since bringin' in the high-priced outsider to exterminate 'em."

"Yeah, Yours Truly has a hunch someone is tampering with Tanker Dan's…"

"Headquarters'll be sendin' new fly swatters soon as da bean counters give da thumbs up. That'll keep da workers movin', and do da job."

Satisfied by Yours Truly's not so truly denial of snooping, Kowolski—maybe because he was on a coffee break, maybe because everyone else at the warehouse was always too busy to gab, or maybe because he wanted to get something off his chest—went on to spill beans like a clumsy hash house waiter:

Cardboard of various thicknesses and strength was made in China, he said. Bulk sheets of the "shit" got shipped around the world to places such as Mexico, where it got cut-and-creased into folded boxes before being flushed into the U.S.A. If any bugs hitched a ride, that was where inspectors should look, the foreman advised, on the borders. The local Red Queen facility was only an undermanned distribution center—operating 24/7 to ship "shit" out rear warehouse truck docks—under constant pressure from headquarters to gin up profits.

♫ *When Rita was bathing in the San Fernando River/ The cockroach stung her/ But she kept on swimming/ La cucaracha, la cucaracha…* ♫

"Ever get any shipments from Venezuela?"

"Yeah, some of da shit sometimes comes in from Caracas via da port in New Orleans, and… I ain't one to bite a hand wit' a sandwich in it," the company man semi-whispered, "but have ya happened to notice that since those Covid bugs got imported from China an' ever'one started stayin' home from work, deliveries of goods to doorsteps in cardboard boxes has become da American way-o'-life?"

♫*People say the cockroach/ is a very small animal/ But when it gets into a house/ It becomes master of it all/ La cucaracha, la cucaracha. . .* ♫

"Don't get me wrong," said the beefy foreman, after gulping down whatever was in the mug. "Dey're hard to spot, but sure, we got a few bugs. Dey seem to like da wormy wood pallets better than da shit, so da profit loss ain't too much. As for big game—rats, raccoons, possums—I ain't sayin' da workers are illegal Haitians or nothin' like dat, but hell, dey'll eat anything."

Then saying that he had to get back to work—drying out shit damaged by a water pipe break—the Red Queen Company foreman reached for the boom box and…

♫**La cucaracha, la cucaracha/ ya no puede caminar/ porque le falta/ porque no tiene/ marijuana que fumar…** ♫

Ankling out of the former factory into fresh air, it occurred to Max that if the current invasion of termites got diverted from the library and houses by easier pickins from China at the Red Star distribution center, it would be what Percy Wilson—in *Case of Daddy Longfellow's Revenge*—called "poetic justice".

♫*My neighbor across the street/ had Lady Claire as her name/ And if she had not died/ she would still be called the same/ La cucaracha, la cucaracha…* ♫

CHAPTER NINE

Claudette Phlegming felt literally chained to her desk. Yes, she had been reinstated, her teacher's salary and benefits had been restored, her well-earned pension was intact. But the union's lawsuit to overturn her wrongful dismissal on trumped-up charges of "inciting a student riot by spouting hate speech" had not freed her to teach. To the contrary, the state's fascist Superintendent of Education had strictly forbidden her to address so-called "controversial subjects" such as genocide of Palestinians by imperialistic Zionists.

For crying out loud, she held four Masters Degrees from prestigious ivory towers, including one from Harvard in Marxist Tactics for Destruction of Western Civilization. In answer to ignoramuses who mouthed the old capitalist cliché that "those who cannot <u>do</u>, teach," she often wore a Teachers Union tee-shirt—imprinted "I Do Do Plenty!"-- to proudly signify her years of filling the empty heads of American youth with enlightened knowledge.

But now—not only was she required to remain silent during so-called Social Studies classes while teenagers robotically repeated capitalist propaganda from assigned state-dictated textbooks—in once-a-month so-called "What Bugs Me" afternoon sessions she was required to listen to petty teenager complaints, and this was one of those monthly periods.

With a sigh, Claudette pointed at a girl in the front row of her classroom, silently signaling that the moronic teenager was to stand and deliver.

"Well, I for one think the 'too cute for school' rule about what students wear is not fair," said the girl wearing an illegal mini-dress no longer in length than a sash in width. "The United States Constant Tutor says we have a right to, uh, pursue happiness. So there, that's what bugs me."

Rahhhhh a few students rahhed.

"Next!" Claudette barked, with a pointed finger aimed at Chela Castro, the brightest student in the class.

"What bugs me is that an insecticidal maniac tows a tanker buggy shaped like a giant insect around town—with 'Good Riddance' printed on it—spreading bad feeling toward termites. During lunch break today a mob at the public library threatened termite extermination!"

Booooo a few students booed.

"Termites should be seen as like people, or what people should be like," Chela continued, while looking down at a notecard. "A famous doctor named Freud called termite mounds perfect examples of, uh, sublimation of individual will to demands of the group. In the words of a Russian revolutionary named Peter, uh, Kropotkin, 'termites are a model, and scientific basis, for Communism.'"

Booooo…

"Silence!" Claudette shouted. "Chela has a right of free propaganda speech!"

"Termite workers live in underground tunnels protected by members of a soldier caste, just like brave Palestinian martyrs that Jews are trying to exterminate."

Rahhhhh…

"Con-tro-verrrsial!" a young male fascist in the back row shouted. But Chela, not to be silenced, bravely stood her ground and… broke out in song:

♫We toilers from all fields united/ Join hand in hand with all who work/ The world belongs to us, the workers/ No room here for the shirk… ♫

Moved to show solidarity with *The Internationale's* sentiments, Claudette herself stood and joined in singing:

♫No more tradition's chains shall bind us/ Arise, ye slaves, no more in thrall/ The earth shall rise on new foundations/ We have been naught, we shall be all ♫

"Workers of the world unite!" her prize student shouted. "You have nothing to lose but your chains!"

Ohhhhh…

"My turn, my turn!" the fat boy in the back row shouted, without being pointed at. "Termites are sorta like Palestinians in Gaza alright. Members of the Hamas 'soldier caste' hide in underground tunnels after making attacks on Israel. But unlike termites, the Hamas 'martyrs' force workers—including women and children—to stay above ground as human shields to Israeli retaliation!"

Ohhhhh…

"Controversial!" Claudette herself retaliated. "Sit down and shut up!"

Ohhhhh…

"'Termites' cause destruction in every place they infest," the teenaged Trumpster nevertheless continued. "Just yesterday my mentor, Mr. Maxwell Morgan, detected that termites broke through defensive extermination efforts at the public library and ate a bunch of American history books. They also undermined the library foundation. Mr. Max fell through the floor, and could have been exterminated himself!"

Ohhhhh…

"According to my Uncle Ralph, a rabbi, the example set by termites is… Well, lots of foreigners come to the United States from wretched countries because of our way of life, but some try to undermine our institutions to make America like the countries they come from, such as, say, Somalia. That violates what's called the Principle of Chesterton's Fence that says people should not tear down something without understanding why it was put in place."

Ohhhhh…

"And Uncle Ralph says that while politicians diddle, malcontents riddle our foundation like termites… infesting the minds of so-called progressives… internet platforms…

the social, entertainment and news media… big international corporations… and especially, so-called academia."

Ohhhhh…

"Ivory towers infested?! How dare your Uncle Ralph, 'the rabid rabbi', make such charges against my many *alma maters!*"

Ohhhhh…

"The idea of democracy, for instance, didn't just grow out of the ground," the mouthy smart aleck ranted, "but lots of fancy *alma maters* have, in effect at least, destroyed the books written by wise men named Socrates, Plato, Aristotle and other philosophers back in ancient Greece and Rome, whose ideas are the foundation of western civilization."

Ohhhhh…

"All old white men!" Claudette thundered. "All deserving to be dumped into the ash bin of history!"

Ohhhhh…

"Academia hasn't dumped Karl Marx, who was an old white man, and Jewish, by the way. Heck, Uncle Ralph graduated from Harvard, but now says his *alma mater's* fight song—*Up the Street*—might as well be…

♫Look where the Crimson banners fly!/ Hark the sound of tramping feet!/There a host approaching nigh!/ Marxists marching on the street/ Harvard strikes home!♫

Booooo…

Though intellectually in solidarity with the cause of, uh, "termites"—theoretically committed to uniting with workers of the world and throwing off the chains of salary, benefits and pension no doubt invested in international capitalism—Claudette sat down and shut up.

CHAPTER TEN

In semi-darkness, Max brought the boiler to a stop at the curb on Redwood Street behind a parked Good Riddance Company tanker buggy. Out of the boiler… across a paved front yard… he stepped onto the porch of a windowless brick house and…

♫I'm a happy termite/ no bigger than a louse/ I live in the tropics/ all around your house/ You hardly ever see me/ I'm so very small… ♫

… detected what sounded like a limbo party going on inside Tanker Dan's residence.

♫Chew, Chew, Chew/ I love those two-by-fours/ Chew, Chew, Chew/ I'll eat your roof and doors… ♫

He knocked on the house's metal front door… waited… knocked again.

♫Chew, Chew, Chew/ I'm a happy termite, who could ask for more?/ Chew, Chew, Chew/ And I love your hardwood floors… ♫

The door opened and…

♫**Those that build with concrete/ they think that they are smart/ Termites can't digest it/ they find it rather tart…** ♫

The off-duty exterminator, wearing pants cut-off at the knees, yellow tee-shirt signed *We Ah Go Party Hard*, and holding a coconut with a straw stuck in it…

♫**So I'll eat your furniture/ And leave all my droppings on your concrete floor…** ♫

"Maximo Morgan? I don't recall inviting you to ah go party, but… Come on in and bust a Gutter Crawler to The Barefoot Boy's calypso classic."

♫**Chew, Chew, Chew/ I love those two-by-fours/ Chew, Chew, Chew...** ♫

A blonde dame—wearing a long bright red, green, gold and black-striped dress, also barefoot and also holding a coconut, introduced herself as Dotty, then held out a platter of crackers that looked to be smeared with the *kumachi* stuff that the Missus Markham cooked up. A little "tart", but...

♫**Chew, Chew, Chew/ I'm a happy termite/ Who could ask for more?...** ♫

"Sorry to break up the festivities, Baldwin," said Max, "but looks like your tip-off about foreign infestation hit a bull in the eye. The town is crawling with termites. And that's not the worst of it."

♫**Orkin man came by today/ Gonna check the house/ His poison will kill anything/ a roach a rat, a mouse...** ♫

"Yeah, we made the national news," said Tanker Dan, with a grin spread across his kisser.

♫**When he let the tent up/ Everything was dead/ except me and my buddies/ We're gnawing on your bed/ Chew, Chew...** ♫

Baldwin flicked a switch to stop the music. Dotty handed Yours Truly a coconut.

"An ex-C.I.A Director on the Rachel Maddow Show said Russian termites attacked the local public library," the insecticidal maniac continued. "Pictures of the damage made it look like we're in a combat zone. And other video showed town folk at each other's throats, half in support of our enemies, believe it or not. Hannity says the termites are Democrats."

"Yeah, Yours Truly doped out that a rack of U.S. History books..."

"Seems an overweight F.B.I. doofus set off the civil strife by falling through the library floor supposedly riddled with undercover invaders."

"Yeah, well, that's why I urgently came by after hours," said Max, ignoring the slightly erroneous news detail. "Ms. Paroo, the library bookkeeper, says you always double-dose the U.S. History area, so Yours Truly has doped out that a certain someone has been diluting your poison to give aid and comfort to the enemies, not only in the library but…"

"No way," said Baldwin, with a glance toward a tank and squirt wand hanging on a coatrack.

"The foreman out at the Red Queen cardboard box joint also says…"

"The bozo cancelled my squirt contract today. He should be investigated by the Feds, and fired."

"Maybe so, but according to the bozo, the warehouse bug problem got worse when you started squirting and the workers laid off swatting."

"Huh," the squirter huhhed. "That sounds like dilution alright," he agreed, with a glance at the wife, Dotty. "But who would, or could do such a thing?"

Grilled by Yours Truly, Baldwin admitted he was "at odds" with his odd family, but, yeah—bingo—came clean that his teenaged brother dropped by from time to time, usually looking for a hand-out. Though never with a girlfriend named Chela Castro, stepdaughter of the foreign haberdasher known as "J. Markham".

"Billy's a good kid, but not the brightest soldier in Ma's mound. "So…"

"So yeah, Yours Truly needs for you to load up the tank with undiluted cyanide, and take on an emergency mission to squirt in the nooks and crannies of our attic, where priceless pulp is stored!"

"Priceless pulp? You mean a private stash of American History books?"

"Nah, much more important materials dating back to, and documenting days and murky nights of *Noir*."

"Not now, Maximo. I've had a hard day and…"

Bang!

The front door—possibly riddled with metal-eating termites—came crashing down!

An armed SWAT squad with *F.B.I.* lettered on obviously bullet-proof vests busted into the house, followed by a typical

G-man wearing a dull gray suit, white shirt, dull gray tie, and flat straw hat.

"This is a raid!" the Fed flatfoot barked. "Special Agent Fass in charge. Anybody makes a false move, they get swatted!"

"Maximo Morgan, licensed private dick," said Max to the bum-steered eager Edgar.

"Oh yeah, we've got the book on you, Morgan. Lower your hands and beat it. This is a Bureau investigation into foreign sabotage of the American way of life that you've already mucked up."

"You've lifted a leg on the wrong hydrant," said Max. "This here is Tanker Dan, the Good Riddance Company's deadly exterminator, who put Yours Truly wise to the foreign plot afoot. A haberdasher—goes by 'J. Markham'—has been smuggling termites into the country, aided and abetted by his Venezuelan Missus, a teenaged stepdaughter and her boyfriend."

"Ha! Markham is a clueless cut-out, set up by this 'here' mug to divert us, and you fell for it, Fatso. The teenagers are also just useful idiots who've been semi-wittingly aiding and abetting."

"Wrong again, Fass. Check that tank hanging on the hatrack over there and you'll detect that its poison contents have been diluted by the teenaged termite sympathizers set on stopping Tanker Dan from ridding the town of infestation."

"Oh, we'll check it alright. And you can take it from me, 'Detective Hong Kong Phooey', the tank's lethal contents will be far from diluted."

The red-in-the-face G-man went on to bluster that Tanker Dan was an underground sleeper...

Underground sleeper?

... one of thousands living undercover as pest controllers, locked and loaded to make a coordinated attack by setting off—not relatively harmless electronic pager bombs like the Israelis did in Lebanon—but much more deadly weapons of mass destruction!

"He's not a ridder, you idiot," said the Junior J. Edgar. "He's a riddler."

Tanker Dan a riddler?

"Termite eggs, wiseguy. Baldwin's assignment was to riddle cardboard at the Red Queen Company warehouse with the tiny 'explosives' before the boxes get sent all over the country. But he's a maniac alright and—carried away with radical revolutionary ideology—started free-lancing around town to stir up civil unrest for what was supposed to be a second phase of the invasion."

"I told you to keep the wand in your pants!" Dotty shouted at her Mister.

"The Bureau's plan was to secretly nab the rogue riddler before rounding up the whole national network," the G-man said. "Thanks to your 'private dickwork', however, thousands of other Chinese operatives have no doubt gone deeper to ground."

Tanker Dan was Chinese?

"Lots of the eggs produce so-called aletes that morf into so-called queens that lay millions more eggs in underground colonies around the country. We've already been infested with a Chinese army of genetically engineered humming bird-size workers and soldiers that—aided and abetted by other useful idiots—are capable of taking down Mount Rushmore."

But... But... But that would be <u>bad</u> riddance!

As SWAT team members started leading the cuffed maniac and his Missus from their nest, Baldwin, smirking, sang:

♫Hark the sound of tramping feet!/ There is a host approaching nigh!/ Marxists marching up the street/ Termites strike home!/ Onward to victory again/ Marching to drumbeat and song... ♫

Good riddance to bad rubbish, in Yours Truly's book. The fake exterminator would be confined for years in a concrete cell at an Iron Bars Hotel, where delicacies such as *kumachi* on crackers would likely not be on the menu. The attic stash of pulp, on the other hand, would not be eaten, not to mention that American History books and the U.S. Constitution would also not be digested. Yeah, Tanker Dan Baldwin had made a big mistake by trying to make Maximo Morgan look useful. But...

♫*I've been hiding in your walls/ And plotting with a mouse...* ♫

Dang it, Max sensed that the devious Chinese riddler had infested his bean with a last laugh of sorts…

♫*I'm hungry/ And I'm going to eat your house…* ♫

… that would likely torment and terrify Yours Truly for years to come.

THE
END

KEEPING IT REAL

A Maximo Morgan Mystery

APRIL

WILLIAM LEROY

WEDNESDAY

April 9, 2025

CHAPTER ONE

At his desk inside a Mister Quickie copy shop workstation cubicle, Max eyeballed the tv screen Quickie had installed for customers waiting on print orders.

As a primetime guy, he'd used to think of daytime boob tube fare as sappy soap operas for broads getting their hair curled at beauty parlors, but…

♫Big Bottom/ Big Bottom/ Talk about bum cakes/ My gal's got 'em… ♫

During a current lull in both Notary Public stamping and private dickwork he'd gotten hooked on re-runs of a reality show featuring a California family of fantastically endowed *femmes* apparently famous for… Well, a couple of months ago a shrink had described Yours Truly as an "ass man" with a so-called fetish for fulsome fannies.

♫Drives me out of my mind/ How could I leave this behind?♫

And something was bound to actually happen today, he suspected, as a bosomy dark-haired babe came on the screen and…

"Hey, Mom," she said to a lookalike older broad, "have you seen my sex tapes lying around? Saint needs something for show-and-tell at school."

"Which one, Sweetheart? The one with Ray J or the one with Kanye or the one… ?"

"Ye and me? No way, Momager. I don't want my little man to catch an Oedipal Complex. And by the way, does this dress make my butt look small?"

"Well, since you asked, yes, it understates your assets, Baby. A thong would be more appropriate for Parents Day."

"The black one or the… ? "

"Are you the 'Fat Man'?" said a female voice from inside the cubicle. "Are you the private detective whose bus-station bench sign advertises satisfaction guaranteed for discreet private investigations?"

With a sigh, Max clicked-off the tv, swiveled his double-wide chair, and detected that a slightly over-ripe redhead had seated herself at the desk across from him.

"Maximo Morgan's the name, and yeah, private dicking is Yours Truly's game," he said to the would-be client. "What's the trouble, Miz… ?"

"For heaven's sake," the broad huffed, "do you live under a rock? *Real Socialites of Oklahoma* has enjoyed nineteen years of popularity."

Oh yeah, his mom watched the weekly show covering the glamorous real lives of another big-city covey of well-to-do broads. But prior to recently "katching up" with Kardashian family re-runs, his firsthand knowledge of reality tv had been limited to a single episode of *COPS*. The one in which Okmulgee County Sheriff's deputies dragged Joe Earl Bennett out of his trailer house west of town and arrested him for indecent assault that—Bennett claimed—was necessitated by the fact that his wife was on fire, and no other source of water was available. So as for *RSOOKers*…

The still unidentified tomato went on to explain that the show's season finale was being filmed on location, also right there in Yours Truly's stamping-and-stomping ground of Henryetta, Oklahoma. And that she had reason to suspect that a plot was afoot to do away with the show's star, a Miss Alice Liddell.

With ears perked up, Max took a small notebook and ballpoint pen from a jacket pocket of his double-breasted suit. Set to grill for case details, he began by asking the client to spell out her name.

"Why, A-l-i-c-e L-i-d-d-e-l-l, of course," she said. "I am the

famous star of the show."

As he continued to grill… Uh oh, domestic disputes spelled t-r-o-u-b-l-e for gumshoes, especially in cases involving bitter custody issues.

Max put down the pen, intending to take a pass and get back to keeping up with what the Kardashian dames were up to, but…

The tv celeb identified an estranged ex-husband by a name that rang a bell loud-and-clear, and said a shooting would likely take place out at the local rodeo grounds at high noon.

Max picked up the pen. He'd had a prior toe-to-toe run-in with the broad's ex, and still had scars to show for the experience. In other words, *Case of a Real Socialite Homicide Plot* would be personal.

CHAPTER TWO

At a vanity inside a shabby room at a hopelessly downtrodden Fountainblue Motel, Dorothy Drew a/k/a Alice Liddell took off her trademark curly red wig and looked into a cracked mirror. Yes, time had taken its dreaded toll, but for crying out loud, she had been a non-stop trouper for virtually her entire life, and for almost twenty years an iconic public personality of social and cultural prominence.

She could have had a conventionally glamorous acting career on stage and/or the big screen; there could be no doubt about that. At the tender age of seven, and the daughter of a typical stage mother, she had hoofed on a local Oklahoma City tv variety show while singing ♫Give my regards to Old Broadway/ And say I'll be there, ere long! ♫ Years of Little Theater had followed, during which she had appeared as Ado Annie in a production of *Oklahoma*, as Roxie Hart in *Chicago* and as Betty Rizzo in *Grease*, to name only a few of her roles.

Upon making it to the Big Apple, however, Pace University's performing arts program had been disappointing. And the lights of the "Great White Way" had dimmed by then. Yes, she had auditioned, but would not have hoofed and sung, unclothed, in a tasteless revival of *Hair* even if she had gotten the part. It was at the nearby lower Manhattan satellite of the British School of Excellence in Etiquette that she honed her acting talent.

Returned to her hometown of Oklahoma City—in addition to social work as a Junior League member—she had gotten a lowly off-screen position at a local tv station. A producer, Bruce Von Mewling, had taken notice of her and… Well, one thing led to another. At the semi-tender age of thirty she was assigned

the "Alice Liddell" persona and selected to host *High Tea With Alice* on a weekly basis. As star of the so-called talk show, she interviewed guests and dispensed etiquette advice on-screen, and by countless personalized thank-you notes to adoring fans *a la* the legendary Emily Post and the great Amy Vanderbilt. When the station announced auditions for a local version of *Real Socialites…*

Knock. Knock. Knock.

Dorothy struck a poised pose of thoughtfully gazing at a wall where a window should have been.

"Here's the script," said her former *Alice* producer and longtime personal assistant, Bruce, rushing into the room. "Brace yourself, my dear."

Dorothy snatched the sheath of papers, put them on the vanity and read:

REAL SOCIALITES OF OK

Episode 12
"Alice Comes to a Reckoning"

After leafing past pages listing cast of characters, shooting schedule, and other information of no interest, she read:

SCENE III

(Organ instrumental of Send in the Clowns. Alice and Faith stand at a rodeo ring fence. They see Rollo pop out of a barrel. They see Angel run to him with a bottle of booze in hand.)

ALICE

Oh dear, handsome as ever after all this time, even with that red nose and unstylish derby hat.

FAITH

Rollo Riggs is the father of your daughter, Alice. And that's her, lighting his fag. Go to them and bury a hatchet.

ALICE

No, my dear, a lady never addresses a gentleman first. Nor shall I drop a monogrammed hankie onto the muddy turf. I shall discreetly leave a

calling card on this fence post and await…
Irritated by the set-up and unrealistic scripted drivel, Dorothy turned the page and read:

SCENE IV
(Organ instrumental of Beer Barrel Polka. Entire regular cast gathered at Ps-'n'-Qs pool hall-'n'-quaint cafe. Intermittent drinking, singing, and laughing by everyone except Alice.)

WANDA
Well, Alice, if you don't want Rollo back, I know someone who would scoot her boots under his bed.

JILL
And her butt into his bunk. Namely you, Wanda. You are such a slut.

ALICE
A cardinal rule of ladylike etiquette is to not notice unwelcome advances, especially when made by uncouth men of prior casual acquaintance.

WANDA
Not notice? You came a hundred miles to this backwater town to see Rollo, and stared right at him and Angel.

JILL
They didn't notice <u>you</u>, Alice. After all these years, to Rollo and your own daughter you might as well be dead.
Dead!
Dorothy frantically thumbed ahead, but…

SCENE VIII
Blank.

SCENE IX
Blank.

SCENE X
Blank!

For crying out loud, *RSOOK* was reality tv. As the show's longtime writer/ director, Larry Davis' job was, yes, to stage situations and spark spontaneous flow of dialogue, but also to provide hints for dramatic plot developments. And since midway through the current season, his "hints" had become increasingly heavy-handed on the subject of death, Alice's death!

Dorothy sighed.

Including Rollo in *RSOOK* at the show's outset had been a mistake. But nineteen years ago she was young, naive, and single. A state fair "Hoofs & Horns Rodeo" was a big Oklahoma City event and Rollo Riggs was said to be a famous star. Bruce, her producer at the time, had invited him to *High Tea*, presumably to, say, demonstrate rope tricks. And Larry Davis, casting for *Real Socialites of Oklahoma* at the time, was a stickler for propriety. One thing had led to another. She was recognized as a real socialite, not realizing until later that she had married a traveling rodeo clown!

Still, it worked for a while, three months to be exact, when "Alice Abandoned Barefoot and Pregnant" emerged as a storyline more credibly in keeping with reality than the more decorous "Toilet Seat Accident" backstory she had suggested. And now, eighteen-and-a-half years later, Larry had reintroduced the clown — along with that incorrigible daughter — for this season's final *RSOOK* episode.

Why?

Was her "reckoning" to be at the hands of the ex-spouse in a tawdry act of cold revenge for that silly long-ago tryst with a door-to-door bible salesman? Was she to be pushed in front of wild animals and trampled to death on the muddy ground of a rodeo ring? Would Larry have Alice written-out of the show with such a tasteless lack of decorum?

Dorothy shuddered. Thought of her demise was unthinkable. In part as the widow of a wealthy oil man — still not re-wed due to spiteful conditions to her rightful inheritance contained in his will — she was the *grande dame* of local high society. Without Alice to herd the current cast of younger feline *femmes*, there

would be no *RSOOK*, but…

Dorothy sighed. Admittedly, ratings were down a bit. Reality needed a boost.

"Take this to a Mr. Morgan at the copy shop down the block," she said, handing the suggested script to Bruce. Services of the overweight private investigator—a man presumably versed in detection of intrigue—were more urgently needed than she had earlier imagined.

In the meantime, she—as "Alice"—would maintain her ladylike composure. Women under duress did not "perspire". They glowed, and conducted themselves with ladylike poise while calmly plotting counter-measures to offensive behavior of others.

CHAPTER 3

Still at his desk, now with his young "Watson" seated across from him, Max put the *Real Socialites of Oklahoma* script aside, and the teenaged case report jotter partly wise to his current lay. In a nutshell, the client would be a sitting duck out at the rodeo grounds.

"Who would want to bump off the star of *RSOOK*?" said the unsavvy kid, who had dropped by during a high school recess and now took a notebook and pencil from a shirt pocket. "According to Aunt Ethel, Ms. Alice is a tireless social worker who has won numerous awards for her good deeds, and is the world's leading authority on etiquette. Her mantra is that it's not what one does, but how one does it."

"Yeah, well, good deeds and polite manners cut no ice in certain social circles," said Max.

"I'll bet it's one of the younger real socialites who's out to get her," said the also overweight pear-shaped kid, a wannabe P.I. who had also studied all the pulp reports and film documentaries of cases handled by famous gumshoes back in the *Noir* and since then. "In the recent *Black Swan* documentary, for instance, a prima donna committed suicide after taking the place of an aging ballet diva—crippled by a suspicious car accident—which proved the younger understudy had a guilty conscience in my book."

"Yeah, but this is Yours Truly's book," said Max. "And in this case…"

"And in Mr. Percy Wilson's famous *Case of An Understudy's Underhand Job,* for another instance," the overly bookish kid continued, "an ambitious young starlet offed a tv show's producer

and pinned the whack job on the show's star.

"In other words, Mr. Max, showbiz is a cutthroat biz, so you'd better watch your step."

"Listen and learn, kid. *RSOOK* is not 'showbiz'. It's reality on tv. The plot afoot has nothing to do with the client being the show's star. And it's personal to Yours Truly."

"What makes it personal, Mr. Max? That's a recipe for pie-in-the-face, you always say."

Max leaned back in his double-wide chair, signaling the kid to commence jotting.

Five years ago a dame blew into town from Frisco, he reported. Trudy Berger, by name. Height, 5' 2". Width, about the same. In other words, a muffin, the kind of dish that made a guy wish he had a butter knife handy. Batting her baby blues, she'd admitted she was on the lookout for a Mr. Right.

He'd started making time. One thing led to another. His mom detected that Trudy was "eating for two" and ordered him to do the right thing. By coincidence, however, the annual Living Legends Rodeo was taking place. And out at the rodeo grounds…

♫*I give 'em a hard ride, then show 'em my backside/ Yeah, a ramblin' rodeo cowboy, that's me…* ♫

Max vividly recalled seeing a long-and-lean cowboy up on a stage, picking a banjo and singing…

♫*I buck 'em and shuck 'em, 'cause who needs their cluckin'/ after a roll in the hay…* ♫

He recalled seeing the endeared look in Trudy's baby blues, not for Yours Truly, but for…

♫*I hump 'em and dump 'em, 'cause who needs their grumpin'…* ♫

He recalled realizing that Trudy's "Mr. Right" was really a love 'em-and-leave 'em Mr. Wrong.

♫*I'm a born rodeo cowboy, and ramblin's my cowboy way…* ♫

"OMG, Mr. Max, was that the lay that led to you… ?"

Yeah, he'd returned to the rodeo grounds the next day, armed with his long-deceased father's old U.S. Army sidearm. He'd spotted the long-and-lean bozo, disguised as a rodeo clown.

Intending only to make Mr. Wrong do right by Trudy…

"You drew down on the 'Ronald McDonald' in front of a bunch of kids and…"

"Well, yeah, it was an accident that luckily…"

"… shot yourself in the foot, literally?"

"… scared Riggs almost as much as the kids."

"But you said it turned out that Miss Trudy's 'Mr. Right' was only a sperm donor," said the kid, returning his pencil to a shirt pocket. "She 'fell for the cowboy' based on a sperm bank profile posted years before."

"A technicality, kid. But yeah, the naive babe knew that Henryetta, Oklahoma is famous for being the rodeo capital of the world, and knew the joker as RR529, obviously an alias for Rollo Riggs."

"So what? To your main squeeze 'RR529' was only a speck of…"

"Riggs a/k/a RR529 is a serial impregnator," Max explained to the clueless teenager. "Turns out he also knocked up a young Ms. Alice Liddell and left her barefoot almost twenty years ago. Now he's back, threatening to knock her off."

"Oh," said the young jotter, retrieving his pencil. "But why would the father of her kid want to rub out Ms. Liddell?"

According to the client, Riggs and she had been in a bitter dispute years ago about custody of their daughter, now a grown-up teenager. Probably the love 'em-and-leave 'em cowboy was a deadly deadbeat dad, desperate to get out of thousands of dollars of delinquent child support payments.

"But again, Mr. Max, you always say that savvy private dicks avoid domestic disputes like low-fat diets."

That was the savvy gumshoe rule alright, but in this case: eye-for-an-eye, tooth-for-a-tooth and…

"What the heck, Mr. Max, you could lose another toe."

Yeah, Yours Truly had a score to settle with Rollo Riggs.

CHAPTER FOUR

Inside a room at the local Fountainblue Motel, Larry Davis sat at a wobbly table, hunched over a laptop computer, fingers poised to take action, but…

Damnit, he was the writer as well as director of *Real Socialites of Oklahoma*, and a writer sometimes had to kill his "darlings". He'd learned that during his first, and only, year of film school almost thirty years ago. The "cutting room floor" was littered with unfilmed characters and unrecorded lines brutally deleted by editorial pens wielded by scribes themselves. Not an easy thing to do, even when scripting fiction. A chilling task when capturing reality.

With a sigh, Larry got up from the table and began to pace.

After exposure to depictions of reality on tv as a teenager, he had become obsessed with catching people on-camera in the act of being themselves when confronted by, say, a naked lady squeezing fruit inside a busy grocery store. If Peter Funt, equipped with only a camera and an eye for the drama of everyday life could do it, so could he.

Out of film school, he'd worked as a lowly grip on the crew of the HBO documentary series called *Real Sex*, helping catch people in the act of being themselves on the phone… in amateur striptease performances… participating in a German game show called *Tutti Frutti* … appearing in Miss Nude pageants… attending a Sex Maniacs Ball to raise funds for crippled children… and sometimes engaging in kinky sexual activities.

But making simple "fly-on-the-wall" documentaries had been unfulfilling. As famously said by a fellow dramatist — the German

one who scripted *Faust*—few people had the imagination for reality. Like tv journalism in general, what people saw on-screen—or even witnessed with their own eyes—had to be framed in interpretive context to be have even minimal effect.

He might have amounted to nothing more than a robotic human camera if not for the flowering of reality tv as a distinct, respected, and wildly popular genre in the new millennium. *Big Brother* and *Survivor*… *The Bachelor* and *Average Joe*… *Wife Swap* and *Who's Your Daddy?*… *The Apprentice*… *The Biggest Loser*… *The Simple Life*… and of course *Laguna Beach: The Real Orange County*. All in one way or another mirrored on-screen not just the words and deeds, but also the dreams and ambitions, the failures and disappointments—in short, the daily dramas—of real people.

Working a gig as writer for a pilot episode of *Busted and Disgusted*, he had set-up a series of situations… A drunken man on a public sidewalk outside a popular bar. . . A stoned lifeguard on the diving board at a country club pool filled with little rich kids… A "pissed off" chef in the kitchen of a swanky restaurant "marinating" a pork loin for an obnoxious diner… all caught on camera inappropriately urinating.

Which had led to him becoming chief writer for *The Anna Nicole Smith Show*, responsible for guiding the famous former *Playboy* Playmate of the Year and wealthy widow of a ninety-year-old Texas billionaire through a series of dramatic personal crises: Deciding that her bedside was the appropriate place to put the share of her recently wed late husband's ashes awarded to her in a bitter court dispute with his son from a prior marriage… Seeking psychiatric help for her pet poodle to stop her—the dog—from humping her—Anna Nicole's—teddy bear… And her ongoing gluttony, as dramatized in a staged eating contest with her lawyer, a slimeball who followed her to a ladies room, listened through the door, and—denying Anna Nicole's claim that she had been taking a dump—accused her of cheating in the contest by intentionally throwing up.

And finally, in 2006 a stroke of good luck: sudden death by

brain stroke of the guy who was to be writer/director of a new *Real Socialites* series set in Oklahoma City.

Larry paused pacing and again sighed.

Some critics—mainly radically militant so-called feminists—criticized *RSOOK* for perpetuating supposedly unrealistic stereotypes of socially active women as "rich, pampered, dependent and hateful toward each other", which was uninformed and unfair. Like all reality—half existential and half perceptive—the "stereotypes" of *Real Socialites* were at least half in the eyes of unsociable feminist beholders.

If anything, perhaps justifying a degree of criticism was his casting Dorothy Drew as "Alice Liddell", a fictional character, literally. Just a name—that of the model for Lewis Carroll's famous "Alice"—adopted by Dorothy for her hosting of an unwatched Sunday morning show on which she blathered nonsensical advice about proper behavior of young ladies. But her unorthodox marriage to a well- known rodeo performer had caught the public's attention and…

Larry again sat down at the wobbly table. He again hunched over the laptop keyboard.

Damnit, as writer/director for *Real Socialites of Oklahoma* he could do with Alice Liddell as he damned well pleased. And had to agree with harsh focus group judgements, merciless social media snarking, *RSOOK*'s declining viewership, and the corner-office suits who held the purse strings: the time had come for the fading star to be written-out of the show.

With that objective in mind, he had gone to a lot of trouble to stage this season's finale in the backwater Oklahoma town famous for rodeos. He'd imagined a dramatic family reunion of Alice, her ex-husband and daughter, with a final shot of the threesome riding into the sunset, so to speak—or maybe not just so to speak— like Steve Martin, Chevy Chase and Martin Short should have done at the ending of *The Three Amigos*.

In the background, Elton John would sing ♫What do you think you'll do then?/ Maybe you'll get a replacement/ There's plenty like me to be found/ Mongrels that ain't got a penny/

Sniffing for tidbits like you on the ground/ So goodbye yellow brick road… ♫

But no, damnit, his Frankensteinian monster was resisting his nudges toward a graceful exit to "pursue other interests" *a la* Kris Kardashian's departure from *KUPWTK*. And he now fully realized that other real socialites, in particular Jill Wadsworth—with whom he had developed a close professional and, uh, personal relationship—would not tolerate a possibility of Alice's return in a later season *a la* the "Momager" of the Kardashian klan.

Hmmm.

Alice would have to meet her Maker. But how? She would not go quietly into that dark night. She would rage at the dimming of the spotlight. And it would be cowardly—not to mention undramatic and possibly dangerous—to simply announce next season that she had died of cancer *a la* the axing of Roseanne Barr in the premiere of *The Conners* series that replaced *Roseanne*. Her remaining fans would rise up in arms. Conspiracy theories would abound. As successor top dog, Jill would be villainized in social and mainstream media. He himself might be attacked for the still somewhat beloved star's death. The show might even be cancelled.

Hmmm.

Much as he'd always aspired to set up and capture on film a graphic facsimile of a death scene—something along the lines of the female swimmer's demise in *Jaws*—the delicate matter would have to be handled indirectly without the victim realizing until the very last moment…

Hmmm.

Maybe the family reunion would not go well. Maybe the estranged ex-husband and daughter held grudges. Maybe…

Hmmm.

A memorable episode of *Seinfeld* came to mind. In one scene: George Constanza's fiancee shown licking glue on envelopes containing invitations to their upcoming wedding… feeling faint. In a following scene: a doctor coming into a hospital waiting room… announcing simply that she was "gone", which was true

to life. The *Seinfeld* actress simply dismissed from the part of the fiancee was disliked by other cast members, and in truth, Alice too had become increasingly difficult to…

Knock. Knock. Knock.

"Go away!" Larry shouted, but… Into the room came *RSOOK*'s executive producer, Luke Stanley, dressed in black jeans, black tee-shirt and black jacket, looking like… like an executive producer.

"I'm working on it," he said to the bean-counter, whose arrival from LaLa Land could mean only one unhelpful thing. "Not to worry, Luke, the season's final episode will be wrapped up on time and on budget."

"Take it easy, *amigo*," said the strictly bottom-line businessman, perching himself on the motel room bed like a… like a black-suited priest, come to administer last rites. "You'll end up killing yourself instead of 'Alice'."

"I'm not a psychopath," said Larry. "To you, 'Alice' is a commodity. To me and the show's audience she is…"

"Yeah, yeah, I know, to you—and to a shrinking audience—she's real. But as a 'person', she was, uh, 'dowdy' from the git-go, to put it kindly."

"'Ladylike' would more kindly describe her. And yes, to me and still thousands of others, Alice is a real, basically good person. Her years of social work for the less fortunate have endeared her to…"

"'Balls', that's Alice Liddell's idea of social work. Fancy parties for her and other women to get dressed-up for. Dinner dances that, after expenses, trickle down pennies to the less fortunate. And whereas her Colbertlike upper-crust affectation was once somewhat amusing, people now take her constant harping on 'which fork to use' as criticism of their real-life trailer-park lifestyles. Criminy, 'not ladylike for a woman to announce her intention to visit a powder room'? Is that reality?"

"She means well, Luke. Her, uh, old-fashioned ways and—okay, her inclination to harp—have a much needed, uh, uncoarsening effect on everyone who watches the show."

"Yes, exactly the problem: her 'good manners' have a chilling effect on the entertainment value of the hair-pulling, literal backbiting and otherwise constant infighting among the other socialites, and… For crying out loud, Larry, you sound like you're in love with Alice Liddell."

Love? Yes, it was that thing called love that had inspired his idea for the season finale, not guilt. Alice's daughter had likely been conceived on his casting couch, he had broken up her marriage to that cowboy, and urged her to give up the newborn for the good of her budding career, all because he had loved her. And in a perverse way, still…

"Larry, get a grip. We have been through this *ad nauseum*."

"Yes, but Alice and I have been through thick-and-thin off-and-on *ad nauseum*," Larry pointed out, rising from his chair. "Her ill-conceived marriage to that cowboy, Riggs. Her…"

"Her pre-conceived pregnancy, as I recall."

"… and her abandonment."

"You yourself wrote Riggs out of the show, and the daughter."

"And let's not forget her understandably critical, but forgiving attitude and helpful harping on the lessons to be learned from the misfortunes of the other real socialites."

"Yeah, yeah, rampant marital infidelities, rapes, abortions, gum disease, sex-change operations, other botched cosmetic surgeries, yada, yada, yada. Ordinary reality has gotten stale, Larry. Television audiences want something new. People want to be shocked. They want to be infuriated. They want to be frightened. They want…"

"Are you kidding? Cable news is circling the drain."

"Reality tv has been blown away by virtual reality, Larry. That's what I came here to tell you. The current *RSOOK* season will be its swan song. The show is to be cancelled, and replaced by…"

Cancelled? Replaced?

"Do with 'Alice' and the others whatever you want," the cut-throat showbiz big shot coldly concluded, before getting up from his perch. "Just keep it within the budget, and don't embarrass all concerned by jumping the shark."

Larry fell face-down onto the bed. Doing away with just Alice would be justifiable homicide. But for Jill and the other socialites to go down with her would be a bloody massacre of innocent victims, including himself.

CHAPTER FIVE

Relieved that rain had forced cancellation of the client's high noon appearance at the rodeo grounds, Max ankled into the Ps-'n'-Qs pool hall-'n'-quaint cafe, furled his umbrella… and put a uniformed security guard who blocked his way wise: Ms. Liddell had called on the blower to personally invite him to the private event in progress. Another *faux* Five-0 checked a list and…

♫… **they hear that oom-pa-pa/ Everybody feels so tra-la-la…** ♫

No doubt due to outside overcast, the cafe barroom was brightly lit, but…

♫**They hear a rumble on the floor-or-or/ It's the big surprise they're waiting for…** ♫

No, a guy with a tv camera hoisted onto his shoulder was on the scene, no doubt part of a news crew from Tulsa.

♫**Roll out the barrel/ We'll have a barrel of fun…** ♫

Celebrity sighting were rare as Democrats in the Sooner State, and according to his teenaged case report jotter's aunt, Alice Liddell was on an A-List of famous broads, along with the Kardashian dames and others named Britney Spears, Lindsay Lohan, Snooki Polizzi, Lil Kim, Mama June and Kaitlyn Jenner.

♫**Roll out the barrel/ We've got the blues on the run…** ♫

After giving the joint a once over, he was further relieved to see that a certain long-and-lean cowboy with the tell-tale red nose of a boozy barroom brawler was not on hand. Otherwise, a gaggle of dressed-up broads yukking it up at the bar—like the Monroe sisters in Percy Wilson's *Case of Family Food Fight*—might have got caught in a crossfire of knuckle sandwiches. Alice Liddell

herself…

♫'**Cause the whole gang is here!** ♫

"Where is Larry?" the client shouted from a spot at the center of the gaggle, while waving a handful of papers in the air. "I need hints for acceptable words."

"He's locked in his room," said one of the other broads, "probably having another nervous breakdown *a la* Woody Allen."

A la Woody Allen?

"He's probably unable to decide whether you should say "c'mere' to, or 'sic'em' at…"

"I shall not speak to, at, or of Mr. Riggs. If one does not have something polite to say about someone, one remains speechless."

"Oh for gawd's sake, Alice," said a younger-looking bleached-blonde skirt, "my mother tells me you started badmouthing Rollo during your wedding ceremony."

"I simply noted that floppy shoes and off-color attempts at humor had no place at the altar, my dear. And during the litigation that followed I was bound by oath to speak unvarnished truth. A paternity test later confirmed what I'd had to say in terms more graphic than I would have preferred."

"But you denied maternity, and refused to submit to a test."

"A lady does not speak of personal affairs, nor tolerate unwelcome prying into private matters. And besides, my dear, as you should well know by now: acknowledgement of parenthood implies unladylike behavior."

Hmmm.

The unusual twist to the custody dispute mentioned by the client earlier put a wrinkle in Rollo Riggs' status as Suspect *Numero Uno* in a possible murrrderrr plot, but…

"Hey, fatso, you're blocking the shot."

Max wheeled around, reached for his shoulder-holstered weapon, but… detected that it was only the news guy, pointing only his camera at the client.

"Mr. Morgan stays in the shot," said Ms. Liddell, grabbing Yours Truly's sleeve and pulling him to beside her. "He is my professional protector, *a la* Kevin Costner in *The Bodyguard*. And

I, *a la* Whitney Houston, have fallen in love with him."

"Never heard of Whitney Houston," said the likely envious bleach-blonde babe, "but springing a surprise 'flirtation' in the season's finale is sure to…"

"I know, my dear, my new love interest is bound to provoke fits of insane jealousy."

"More like shock, especially after seeing how deep into the barrel you've delved."

Max was not surprised by the predictable turn of events. Private dicks since back in the times of *Noir*—from Mike Hammer to Phillip Marlowe to Sam Spade—had always been chick magnets. Mindful, however, of Charlie Chan's *Case of a First Lady's Secret Service*—and Chan's observation that "combining affection with protection leads to erection interference", or something like that—he attempted, unsuccessfully, to free himself from the client's clutches.

"And for crying out loud, Alice, last season you copied Khloe K and claimed that Black professional wrestler—'Bevis the Beaver Cleaver'—was your 'Mr. Right'. This is reality tv, 'my dear', and you are a bit long in the tooth for 'intimate relations'. The only credibly romantic sub-plot in play involves me and…"

"Yes, my dear, my many fans have besieged me with correspondence confirming my suspicions that you have been indiscreetly conniving on the off-camera casting couch to replace me as *RSOOK's* star. I have engaged Mr. Morgan to expose the plot in all its tawdry detail, and to take a bullet for me if necessary."

Take a bullet?

"How dare you snoop on me!" the bleach-blonde bimbo screeched, lunging at the client with bared bright red claws.

"Hold your water, Sweetheart," said Max, edging himself between the two real socialites. "Ms. Liddell is doing you a favor by hiring Yours Truly. Rollo Riggs is a love 'em-and-leave 'em serial impregnator."

"I know that. He 'loved' and left Alice barefoot-and-pregnant in Season One, when I was only a teenager. So what?"

"Yes, Mr. Morgan, what has that rodeo clown to do with your investigation into off-camera shenanigans that threaten me?"

"Well, it's early days, but Yours Truly has the book on Riggs and…"

"Forget him and your book. It is none other than Larry Davis who holds the poison pen."

Larry Davis? The joker previously referred to as *a la* Woody Allen?

Max recalled crossing paths with the real Allen five years ago — coincidentally while making time with Trudy Berger — and now couldn't help thinking of the creep as depicted in the educational dvd Trudy brought by for "popcorn-and-Netflix" on the den sofa, as the kid would put it. Yeah, weird: in the documentary titled *All You Ever Wanted to Know About S-e-x, But Were Afraid to Ask*, Allen was disguised as a sperm cell. And Trudy had explained that he was part of a gang, half of which were "hitmen" who mercilessly bumped off members of other gangs competing for women's "eggs".

In other words, sight unseen in real flesh, Max pictured a Larry Davis as a murderous hitman in hardball competition with Yours Truly.

CHAPTER SIX

Cuckoo. Cuckoo. Cuckoo.

A little bird incorrectly announced the time of Alvin "Butch" Kilpatrick's return to the home appliances-and-tools repair shop owned and operated by him and his wife, Fergie. Though soaked to the bone, he passed by a narrow staircase leading to their second-floor living quarters, limped directly to his workbench and took down from a wall one of an array of framed photographs, each personally signed by…

"She stood you up, didn't she," said the wife, eyeing him from behind a counter where she was tending to repair of a cuckoo clock. "She saw you—a hunchbacked, clubfooted, walleyed freak—and left you standing in the rain with a stupid look on your face. I warned you not to try to make it real."

Cuckoo.

Alice had not "stood him up", at least not exactly. Her scheduled appearance at the local rodeo grounds had been cancelled due to rain. Even worse, however, with his nose pressed against the window of the Ps-'n'-Qs pool hall-'n'-quaint cafe, he'd seen her take the arm of the fat man who worked as a Notary Public at Mister Quickie's copy shop. He'd read her lips, telling one and all that she had fallen in love with the previously unsuspected rival for her affections.

So yes, he'd been made to look like a fool, Butch admitted to his longtime spouse, from whom he kept no secrets.

Almost twenty years ago, within days of returning from a weekend honeymoon, their marriage had become stale. Desperate for a fresh relationship, he had become romantically enthralled

with the real Oklahoma socialite, Alice Liddell. Divorce from Fergie was out of the question for both religious and practical reasons. And during a fifty minute online marriage counseling session, at a cost of almost two hundred dollars, the situation had been explained and resolved to their mutual satisfaction.

At an early version of the *Doctor On Demand* website a veterinary psychologist had pointed out that in males of many species passion for not only jealous vengeance but also romance was enflamed by awareness that a mate was engaging with another. And sauce for the gander, sauce for the goose, a female associate had added. Females of many species subconsciously promoted competition for "fatherhood of their offspring", as indicated in part by the inclination of married women to have extramarital affairs during their periods of "estrus".

Cuckoo.

In a refreshed marriage arrangement, not exactly "open" but "ajar", he had continued to carry on with Alice Liddell from afar. The wife had taken up with Phil Harris, a swashbuckling ship captain and crab catcher on the *Deadliest Catch* reality tv show. As predicted by Dr. Phil's online associates, the resulting "hysterical bonding" between Fergie and him had been mutually blissful. And after Harris suffered a brain stroke during an especially deadly episode, his dying words were that "the show must go on."

Following a brief period of unblissful mourning, Fergie had outfitted herself with fresh lingerie, new toys, and started what turned out to be a two-year relationship with a guy named Duane, better known as "Dog" on *Dog the Bounty Hunter*, during which their marital love life again sizzled. Since then, her affairs with Dr. Terry Dubrow on *Botched*, Si Robertson on *Duck Dynasty*, Todd Crisley on *Crisley Knows Best* and other reality tv stars—not to mention a memorably steamy one-night stand with the short guy, Matt Roloff, star of *Little People, Big World*—had kept the home fires burning. Currently she was involved with Buckin' Billy Ray Smith, an *Ax Men* star.

He, on the other hand, had remained extramaritally engaged exclusively with Alice, even when she…

Cuckoo.

"It wasn't me who crossed the line," said Butch, taking down another photo, the one dated February 14, 2012 and signed *With fond regards, Alice Liddell.* He had not driven the ninety miles to Oklahoma City where Alice lived as a real socialite. He had never "stalked" his semi-secret significant other. He knew the Dr. Phil rules, but… but… Alice knew from his many letters where he lived.

"She came to Henryetta of her own free will," he shouted. "Alice is the one who wanted to… to…"

"To make you jealous, Alvin. She's feeling neglected. It's competition for a woman's favors that makes a manly lover's heart beat fast."

Well, yeah, his competition with famous tv stars for Fergie's favors was a turn-on. And truth be told, his hots for Alice had heated up during her occasional, uh, flirtations with other men during a few *RSOOK* episodes. But…

"No way do I forgive and forget," he declared. "Not this time. Her 'flirtations' with that plumber in Season Eleven, with that twitchy one-armed paperhanger in Season Fourteen, and last year' with the Black WWE star may have been innocent, but this time… No way am I going to compete in the flesh with that local fat man."

"Fine, but just keep in mind how those prior little spats with Alice affected our relationship? There are two of us in this ajar marriage, Alvin. Just as you need a hot wife to think of yourself as a cool guy, for my heart to beat fast I need to think of you as desirable to another."

Cuckoo. Cuckoo.

He would get involved with one of the Kardashian sisters, he promised. Kim was back on the market, and this time…

"Ha! Kim didn't answer any of your letters. She never even thanked you for that ham you sent her for a Christmas."

Though painful to admit, his wife was right. Except with Alice, he'd not had much luck with women. But passing notes with… Okay, Alice was all the time mentioning her social work with

a group called the Junior League. He'd looked up the women's organization online and found… Heck, the claim that Junior Leaguers never joined orgies because of the number of thank you notes they would be <u>obligated</u> to write must have been a joke. Alice wrote to him, not because she had to, but because…

"Grow a pair Alvin," the wife advised. "Show Alice—and me—that you are a man driven by passion. Fight for her. Otherwise, well, you know what doesn't happen when my heart beats slow."

Yeah, he knew: the wife's temperature dropped to below zero. Marriage became miserable.

Alvin donned a pair of thick googles and, picturing the fat Notary Public in Alice's embrace, began to passionately peddle with his good foot. As the stone wheel mounted to his workbench began to whir, he took in hand an ax he'd been working on, and began to passionately sharpen its blade.

Cuckoo. Cuckoo. Cuckoo. Cuckoo. Cuckcoo…

CHAPTER SEVEN

"Yes, the real housewives are in town for an episode, and Max is going to be in this week's show."

Max, at the kitchen table inside the house they had shared since his birth, dug into a second serving of peach cobbler as his mom, on the blower—even without knowing that Alice Liddell had fallen for him like a new bride's honeymoon nightie—continued to brag about his *RSOOK* gig.

"Yes, believe it or not. Max is to be Alice's 'bodyguard'. Ha, ha, ha…"

As longtime fan and regular watcher of the reality tv show, Mom had been excited about him becoming a celebrity, but now, dang it…

"Oh no, ha, ha, ha, but… Well, yes, he does have the, uh, bulk to stop a bullet, or even a bazooka shell fired at her. Ha, ha, ha…"

And though a big fan of the old documentary movie, *The Bodyguard*, she now also seemed to be having a hard time seeing him as *a la* Kevin Costner in the case of a diva being stalked by a would-be killer.

"Larry Davis is the show's director, and has been giving Jill Wadsworth a lot more attention than she deserves," his mom was saying to her sewing club chum, Cora Oakley. "A shadow of Larry, skulking, comes on-screen from time to time. And occasionally the camera catches him ogling her like a butcher sizing up a fresh fryer."

Yeah, like the client, Mom sounded suspicious that the dolled-up bleach-blonde real housewife named Jill was not only carrying on with Davis, but also angling to take the starring role

in *Real Socialites of Oklahoma.*

"No, the tall bald one is Alice's devoted personal assistant, Bruce. Larry Davis is the wimpy Woody Allen lookalike. Max suspects he is plotting to 'rub out' Alice. Ha, ha, ha…"

Max pushed the peach cobbler aside.

Dang it, *RSOOK* was reality tv. In the show's season finale he would not be a clueless "Barney Fife" in a fun-and-games episode of *Mayberry RFD.* But his mom seemed not to realize—and neither had it fully dawned on him until just now—that he might be exposed to real danger in a line of fire, not as Alice Liddell's private dick, but by her identification of Yours Truly as both her new main squeeze and bodyguard.

CHAPTER EIGHT

Up from the motel bed after a long cry and short nap, Larry again sat hunched over his laptop. He had been blindsided by Luke Stanley's announcement that *RSOOK* was to be cancelled, and replaced. Now he had only twenty-four hours to catch up, and though he usually disdained so-called entertainment industry news...

At *Deadline*'s website, Larry went to the TV Section, scanned current headlines...

TRUE CRIME PAYS OFF BIG ON NETFLIX
NBC GREENLIGHTS GAZA GAME SHOW
MENENDEZ BROS MUSICAL IN WORKS

... glanced at a few others of no interest and moved on.

At *Vulture*, he read that Kim Kardashian and Kanye West had been seen in public, though not together... that Kris Kardashian and Caitlyn Jenner had not been seen in public, but were rumored to be back together. . . that all the Kardashians were getting together for a publicity stunt on Fathers Day ... and there it was, like a slap in the face:

STANLEY & STANLEY VS. DISNEY
RACE TO BOTTOM

Rumors that Stanley & Stanley Productions intend to take on Disney's recently announced new reality tv series—called **On the Rag**—*were confirmed during a recent sit-down with S&S Executive Producer, Luke Stanley:*

Vulture: *Almost twenty years ago, Lily Allen explained her hit song, The Fear, as inspired when she woke up one morning and shouted "This is wrong!" at the tv screen. She explained that she feared there*

was not going to be anything real in the world that isn't sponsored. Now rumor has it that S&S intends to "jump the snark", so to speak, and further blur what's real on tv. So what exactly is your new reality tv concept, and how can you hope to top, or rather, sink lower than Disney's reported line-up of nasty celebrities.

Stanley: *Smart cookie, Miss Allen, who achieved musical fame via social media. In her hit song, as I recall, she admits she wants diamonds despite hearing that women die trying to find them. And that she herself would be "shameless", 'cause everyone knows that's how you get famous. On the other hand, Disney's* **On the Rag** *is just a warmed-over version of The View, as evidenced in part by its line-up of that Black lawyer, What's-Her-Name Hostin, a real bitch, yeah, but not a real celebrity.*

Vulture: *Yes, but with Amy Schumer, Meghan Markel, Ellen DeGeneres and other snarkers in the same room — not to mention Don Lemon — there's bound to be an entertaining non-stop catfight.*

Stanley: *All has-beens and never-wases. Social media is what people with pulses are into. In our new series — to be called either* **Snark Tank** *or* **Freak Show**, *but that's off the record for now — we'll tap into the vast audience of current social media addicts, and also bring to reality tv what the billions of pissed-off people still not online have been missing.*

Vulture: *Such as exactly what?*

Stanley: *Insane rants on topical subjects by former moderators of banned Reddit accounts such as r/Coontown… r/FatPeopleHate… and r/UpYours. All certified psychopaths, sociopaths and other pathetically maladjusted misfits. Picture an all-girl WWE free-for-all cage match with no holds barred.*

Vulture: *Sounds exciting.*

Stanley: *Yeah, plenty of toxic snarking to entertain viewers, not just influencers such as knocked off family shows such as The Duggans that gave reality entertainment a bad name. Our cast of freaks will indiscriminately vent rancid racism, abhorrent anti-semitism, agism, ableism, cruel lookism and violent vigilantism in all directions. They'll snipe at, doxx, and bitch about everyone, especially each other. Viewers will be able to text or call to join the fun. And we'll be live,*

so who knows what might happen.

Vulture*: Well, yes, that's why many industry observers are worried that spewing of unmitigated hate might spark…*

Knock. Knock. Knock.

Larry got up from the laptop, went to the door, and — expecting much needed "room service" by Jill Wadsworth… Oh no, barging into the room came *RSOOK*'s temperamental star, Alice Liddell, looking especially, uh, temperamental.

"We need to talk," she said, before sitting down on the rumpled motel bed and, oh no, lighting a cigarette, a sure sign that her alter ego…

Larry chained the door and prayed Jill would not come knocking.

"I saw that asshole from Stanley & Stanley leave your room, and…"

"Don't say things like that!"

"… I know you're under pressure to goose ratings. So I got to thinking: Larry, you can't kill Alice."

"I don't want to, believe me. But…"

"Yeah, yeah, I know: Jill has been 'servicing' your perverted needs. Been there, done that, and…"

"Alice would never be so vulgar as to even allude to…"

"Larry, this is 'Dorothy' talking: Make Jill a star and you'll find yourself in the position of the proverbial groom following marriage to a proverbial Jewish princess. No more blow jobs."

"Stop it! You are Alice, and… and you don't smoke cigarettes in the presence of others!"

"Yes, I am Alice," said the fading star, leaning to dunk the butt in a bedside glass of water. "And I will always be Alice. If you get rid of me and I have to move on with my career to play, say, Lady McBeth on-stage…"

"Lady Macbeth! Ha! You'll have no career. In addition to lack of talent, you're as indelibly typecast as Lassie back in the day. That's showbiz, my dear."

"Exactly my point, Larry. If nothing else, I will still be famous. People will see me on the street, alive and well. They'll think

RSOOK <u>was</u> 'showbiz'. Your reputation and career in reality TV will be in the crapper."

Larry winced. Though obvious, the complication pointed out by... by Alice had not occurred to him. But he had made promises to Jill and...

"Kill <u>her</u>," said... Dorothy Drew. "She will go on to be a nobody, nothing but a run-of-the-mill bleach-blonde ex-socialite, a nobody that no one will remember or recognize on the street."

Hmmm.

"Make it look like murder to end this season as a whodunnit. I have already hired a private detective, and next season..."

"A private detective!"

"Hell's bells, a 'Who shot J.R.' storyline famously carried a popular 1980s soap opera through an entire season and into television lore."

Hmmm.

Told that he would think about "shooting" her rival, Alice Liddell a/k/a Dorothy Drew and/or Dorothy a/k/a Alice peaceably departed.

Larry returned to the laptop... finished reading the *Vulture* article about Stanley & Stanley's new reality tv concept and... as fate would have it, noticed another headline...

USC TO HONOR SHELDON MEYER WITH PhD

... and following article:

The late writer/director, Sheldon Meyer is to be posthumously awarded an honorary doctorate from the University of Southern California (USC) School of Cinematic Arts in recognition of his pioneering body of work that many would describe as cinema verite (sometimes called observational cinema), a style of filmmaking that combines improvisational use of the camera to unveil truth or highlight subjects hidden behind reality. And he did it all on the cheap.

With only $16,000 in their pockets, Meyer and his longtime colleague, Gene Hoffman, decamped from Hollywood to Miami in1957. Like others on the South Florida scene freed from stifling oversight, they started Stupendous Pictures with a string of so-called "nudie cuties", featurettes that managed to avoid censors' knives by

use of dexterous advertising. Billed as either educational hygienic shorts or nature films, they were really what most would call blatant exploitation films. **Tawdry Tina's Big Night** *was the first five reels of 16mm sleaze distributed by Stupendous to grindhouses and drive-in movie theaters across the land.* **Dirty Nurses, Bambi's Birthday, The Libidinous Ones** *and numerous others followed. Biz was good.*

Until 1962, when the legendary duo of Herchell Gordon Lewis and David F. Friedman — having sensed that a new taboo had to be breached if eentertaining xploitation was to survive and prosper — came out with **Blood Feast.** *Overnight, blurry, hand-held close-ups of erect nipples and bushy crotches were passe. Audiences — outraged, shocked and horrified by sight of bloody <u>internal </u>body parts — ate up the gore and demanded more. And by happy happenstance, capturing on film the starkest of reality had always been Sheldon Meyer's obsession.*

The result for posterity: **Crimson Orgy,** *a cult classic. For Meyer: a nervous breakdown, and fifteen years after shooting the film's final scene, death by shooting himself … in the head… with a shotgun.*

In recognizing **Crimson Orgy** *as possibly the first, perhaps only genuine "splatter film" (sometimes referred to as "snuff film"), faculty members of the USC School of Cinematic Arts cite the Meyer opus as inspiration for filmmakers seeking the ultimate artistic achievement of inducing catharsis, but also as a cautionary…*

Unable to make himself read more, Larry slammed the laptop shut.

He himself had seen a vcr copy of a 76-minute cut of Sheldon Meyer's supposedly "lost masterpiece" of visceral horror: an ordinary low-budget bloodbath of poorly staged gruesomeness, notable not really for its a famous final scene — depicting a young woman's cleavage by buzzsaw — but for the aspiring starlet's actual, likely unrelated accidental death during the filming that suggested ultimate reality had been captured on film. Otherwise, *Crimson Orgy* would have been deservedly long forgotten even if briefly noticed.

Damnit, with any such luck, he himself — Larry Davis, USC drop-out — coulda, shoulda and woulda been the recipient of posthumous kudos.

THURSDAY

April 10, 2025

CHAPTER NINE

Following a sleepless night of tossing-and-turning, Max ankled into Quickie's to pick up his heater, just in case. Except for his long-deceased father's old military sidearm that he kept for sentimental reasons, Roscoes were not allowed at home, not even his exact replica of Mike Hammer's "Old Junior" that did not actually squirt lead. Just flashing the fake .45 would hopefully be enough if…

Hello, the kid had already parked his big backside in the client chair. Before Yours Truly could do likewise in his own double-wide seat…

"I got to talking with Uncle Ralph about our current lay," said the young case report jotter, "and he thinks the threat against Ms. Liddell…"

Max held up a hand to signal stifle.

"What?" said the kid. "Have you got the goods on that serial impregnator, Mr. Max?"

"Nah, Riggs got custody of the daughter, so has no reason to have his red nose out of joint."

"Aha! An understudy is in the frame, right? Just like in Mr. Percy Wilson's *Case of*…"

"Nah, turns out there's another would-be doer in the picture and…"

"A Stan! Yep, Uncle Ralph, a rabbi, is almost always right."

Stan?

"Eminem's term for a 'stalking fan'. You know: ♫I got a room full of your posters and your pictures, man/ Hit me back, just to chat/ Yours truly, your biggest fan/ This is Stan ♫

Max recalled the M&M jingle as more along the lines of ♪M&Ms spells mmm mmm, that's the sound when you eat 'em ♪, but let the irrelevant detail slide.

"A plain stalker," the kid continued, "would be someone such as the broad who threatened the famous actress, Catherine Zeta-Jones—with calls and letters saying she would "cut up" the famous movie star and "feed her to dogs"—only because she, the female stalker, was infatuated with the victim's husband, who is also a celebrity."

Dang it! Ms. Liddell said on tv news that her identification of her new "love interest"—namely, Yours Truly—was bound to provoke a fit or insane jealousy. In other words, yeah, Yours Truly would now be the target of a deranged stalker.

"Stans", on the other hand, directed their threats to the idols they adored, and were Celebrity Enemies *Numero Uno*, according to the kid, who then explained that he had followed up on his uncle's tip with an hour of Google research. "Obsessed fans think words spoken or sung by their idols for a mass audience—especially romantic words—are personally for them. They confuse illusion with reality, feel a false closeness with the real person, and when making contact in real life often if not usually end up feeling dissed."

Double-dang it!. A "Stan" theory of the case would not only put Yours Truly personally in crosshairs, but—in addition to Davis—would open up multiple possibilities of threats to the… to the reality tv star, which could catch Yours Truly in a crossfire.

As Max stewed in sweat… Murder of a member of the famous Beatles quartet was the classic case involving a Stan, said the Googled-up teenager. And almost all celebs dealt with the threat at one time or another, especially dames: A famous Selena Somebody and a Christina Grimmie both got killed by Stans. Another Stan who was making moves on a celebrity named Madonna—after writing her a note threatening to "slash her throat from ear to ear" if she turned down his marriage proposal—assaulted a well-armed <u>bodyguard</u> that had to plug the mope in self defense!

Max got up from the desk. Old Junior would be useless against a jealous dame-dizzy maniac and... He had taken on Alice Liddell as a client only to detect evidence proving his hunch that her estranged ex-husband was out to get her, then turn the case over to the cops and D.A. And... And... And the *RSOOK* star herself had instead fingered the show's writer/director, Davis .. and could herself now go to police. To investigate a multitude of possible suspects would take a nationwide F.B.I. dragnet.

In a nutshell, Yours Truly was a professional gumshoe, not a hired goombah. He'd not signed up to be a bodyguard "*a la* Kevin Costner", and possibly take a bullet for... just a client. Nor had he willingly become Ms. Liddell's "love interest", and possibly the target of a misguided jealous rival.

CHAPTER TEN

Alice strolled from the Fountainblue Motel toward the Ps-'n'-Qs pool hall-'n'-quaint cafe, escorted by her ever-attentive personal assistant, Bruce Von Mewling, and by the *RSOOK* Best Boy, Marty Somebody. Lack of fan demand for the personally autographed head shots carried by Bruce was disappointing, but—on the brighter side—the updated script skimmed by her and now carried by Marty was promising.

According to the Best Boy, Larry had viewed yesterday's footage into wee hours, and liked what the camera had "captured" in his absence. So the previously scripted rodeo grounds scene involving her ex-husband and that daughter of his had been scrubbed. Instead, the barroom scene—in particular the dramatic tension that had arisen between her and Jill Wadsworth—was to be further developed.

Had the chronically equivocal *RSOOK* writer/director heeded her demand that Jill—not she—be terminated for the good of the show?

Inside the cafe, lights were already blazing in the bar area. The other real socialites were already assembled, and for continuity—though the hour was in fact early—were already consuming alcoholic beverages. The overweight detective, however, seemed to have missed the crew call, which was annoying and slightly worrisome. Also Larry…

"The Boss says to go ahead without him," the Best Boy shouted from behind a cameraman. "Let's roll."

♫**Roll out the barrel/ We'll have a barrel of fun…** ♫

Alice glanced again at the script, put on a bright smile, and

stood her ground, forcing Jill to come to her and the cameraman to adjust his angle.

♫Roll out the barrel/ We've got the blues on the run… ♫

Other real socialites, except for Jill, broke into fake laughing.

♫'Cause the gang's all here!♫

But before she could speak her first lines…

"You're a fine one to be gossiping about casting-couch 'shenanigans'," her opposite number screeched. "Everyone knows your own long-ago 'audition' consisted of you banging Larry off-camera, then tricking that cowboy clown into making you look respectably married. And now you're at it again, trying to trick Larry into…"

"Cut!" Alice shouted in the Best Boy's direction. "The script suggests that this… this person simply deny that she is in fact 'banging' Larry in a pathetic attempt to have him terminate me! If Mr. Morgan were here, he would no doubt have evidence by now that proves she has been plotting…"

"Okay, Ms. Liddell," said the Best Boy in his slightly deeper "assistant-director's" voice. "Let's leave the catfight for Larry, and in the meantime shoot your monologue."

Given a minute to review the script, Alice went to a relatively quiet corner and, while pacing, read:

SCENE

IV*

(continued)

(Alice looks directly into camera. The song Lady Macbitching Beth plays softly in background.)

ALICE

Sometimes it is difficult to be a lady. When confronted by especially offensive vulgarity of others, wanting to look like an innocent flower and be a serpent underneath, I myself—a graduate of the British

School of Excellence in Etiquette—sometimes wish I could shed my refined femininity and cruelly retaliate without pity. Men in such situations, especially well bred gentlemen, are free—indeed bound by honor—to strike down vulgarians by whatever means necessary. And to quote the Bard, when 'tis done, 'twere well it were done quickly.

Though a bit overwrought, the scripted words were basically in accord with her—and, Larry's?—view of what had to be done about Jill Wadsworth, but... When push came to shove, would the mousy writer/director screw his courage to the sticking place? That was the question. Larry was not without ambition. He desperately aspired to greatness, but so far—like the cat in the famous saying—had wanted to eat fish without getting his feet wet. The season finale was half done and...

"Pardon me for interrupting your mumbling, Ms. Liddell, but we need to talk."

"Mr. Morgan, at last. Pray tell, what damning conclusions have you come to so far?"

"Only that Yours Truly will not be able to be your bodyguard *a la* Kevin Costner after all."

"But I remain in danger, and our agreement provides..."

"And neither will I be able to be your love interest from now on."

"Pray tell, why not?"

"Well, just between the two of us, yeah, I'm a private dick, but 'Old Junior' doesn't actually squirt lead."

"How dare you speak to me of such matters!"

"For run-of-the-mill gumshoeing I usually just flash the Roscoe, but..."

"You shall do no such disgusting thing in my presence. But shall nevertheless continue to provide regular 'run-of-the-mill' private investigative services through tonight's wrap of the season finale, for which you have already been paid."

"Ms. Liddell, please, you yourself have already identified the Davis dude as the *a la* Woody Allen wouldbe hitman," the cowardly "gumshoe" whined. "So now..."

"Mr. Allen is seldom a 'hit man', and I have put on hold my

suspicions regarding Mr. Davis."

"Okay, but if a stalker and/or a Stan thinks bodyguarding and/or Netflix-and-popcorn is going on, he or she might…"

Various types of on-set incidents were common, Alice pointed out. Investigation was often needed, and "when 'tis done, 'twere well it were done quickly."

"Incidents?"

For instance, the famous actor, Alec Baldwin, shot and killed a female camera operator a couple of years ago during the filming of a movie.

"Yeah, I read about that. The other dame responsible for loading the gat with blanks took the rap and Baldwin skated."

"Just between you and me for now, Maxie," said Dorothy, "in the event any such incident occurs during the shooting of this season's *RSOOK* finale, the powers-that-be are already planning to peg an entire next season around an ongoing investigation of what happened and who done it, in which case you would be a co-star."

With that detail settled and… one of Larry's stirring musical intros beginning to faintly play, Dorothy returned to the brightly lit cafe bar area and informed the Best Boy sitting-in as director that she was ready to recite her monologue.

"It's never too difficult to be a lady," she then barked into the camera. "When confronted by especially offensive vulgarity such as often displayed by Jill Wadsworth, a lady might for a moment wish she were a man. Instead, she retains her refined femininity and restrains herself from justifiably retaliating against a churlish deplorable, who may look like a wilting flower but is a serpent underneath. It's up to real men to strike down vulgarians by whatever means necessary. And given that this is the season's final episode, when 'tis done, 'twere well it were done quickly."

CHAPTER ELEVEN

Nudged into the spotlight by his co-star, Max looked into the camera, took a deep breath, and—for the benefit of any insanely jealous Alice Liddelll fans out there in reality tv land—explained loud and clear:

"Maximo Morgan is the name, private dicking—not bodyguarding and not serving as the client's main squeeze *a la* Kevin Costner—is Yours Truly's game. The lay is only to investigate any incidents that might occur during this season's final *Real Socialites of Oklahoma* episode, and return next season to tie-up loose ends. Hopefully…"

"Incidents?" the bleached-blonde real socialite shrieked. "What now, Alice? What publicity stunt have you concocted in another desperate attempt to save your career?"

"How dare you suggest I would sully my true life story with a cheap 'stunt'!" Ms. Liddell huffed, but…

"Ha! Your entire *RSOOK* career has been nothing <u>but</u> a series of cheap publicity stunts to promote your so-called educational products about 'etiquette', your paid extra-curricular speaking engagements, and your overblown ego," the het-up real socialite likely named Jill Wadsworth continued. "Let us re-count the trite ways in which you have prostituted yourself:

"Marriage to a celebrity, though a minor one… 'Immaculate conception' of a daughter… Abandonment and contentious divorce… Drawn out child custody litigation… Multiple 'flirtations', including the one with a pre-teased 'guest star' bribed to boost ratings, who turned out to be the local weatherman, for crying out loud."

"Gary 'Jumping Jack Flash' Ireland broke my heart when he ran off with that trashy storm chaser," said the client. "But yes, the outpouring of emotional support from my many fans during Season Five was quite, uh, uplifting."

Hmmm.

Max, though not a fan of Encyclopedia Brown, recalled the famous boy detective's *Case of the Missing Statue*, in which a famous actress purchased the main prop of her recently released movie — titled *The Stolen Statue* — then reported an actual theft of the piece in a sensational incident headlined "life imitating art". Her bodyguard backed up her story that a huge man had overpowered him, tied a string of ripped-up bedsheets to a bed, and used the makeshift rope to escape with the statue through a second-floor window. But...

"So again, what's next, Alice? Your survival of a staged assault, robbery and kidnapping by masked thugs *a la* Kim K's much publicized ordeal, perhaps juiced up by your tearful account of them conveniently shouting 'This is MAGA country!'?"

"A lady never engages in controversial commentary about contentious political matters."

"Maybe your overweight love interest will 'accidentally' leak a steamy sex tape of the two of you..."

"Mr. Morgan!" his co-star barked. "Don't just stand there with your mouth agape! Defend my reputation by... Flash your Roscoe if you must..."

"To repeat, Yours Truly is no longer Ms. Liddell's love interest!"

"... to put a stop to this... this unseemly scene before it provokes an unfortunate incident."

"Trite, but appropriate, Alice," said the blonde. "You've been 'going down' for years, and have now reached the bottom."

Hmmm.

Max now recalled that in *Case of the Missing Statue*, young Brown tossed the rope of bedsheets out the second-floor window and called for his buddy — Bugs Meany — to climb up and meet the famous movie star. When Bugs started to climb, bingo, his weight moved the bed to which the sheets were tied. So yeah, a

huge man could not have made off with the also weighty statue. In other words, the report of reality imitating art was a publicity stunt staged to promote a movie, and its star.

Hmmm.

Max wondered: Was his client, Alice Lindell—like Sam Spade's client in *Case of the Maltese Falcon*—a *femme fatale*? Was Yours Truly—like Spade—being played for a sap?

Hmmm.

CHAPTER TWELVE

Each man kills the thing he loves/ By each let this be heard…

Lingering in bed, dreading the grisly task of snuffing the professional lives of all the real socialites, Larry sensed his Muse—the creative goddess within him—begin to stir.

He had long felt a spiritual kinship with Oscar Wilde, a fellow scriptwriter as well as author of the famous poem—*Ballad of Reading Gaol*—about a man condemned to death for the murder of a beloved woman.

Some do the deed with many tears/ And some without a sigh…

Up from the bed and in the shower, he flashed on the famous death scene in Alfred Hitchcock's classic film, *Psycho*:

At a seedy out-of-the-way motel not unlike this one a youngish woman—her figure not unlike that of Jill Wadsworth—flushing bits of paper down the round hole at the bottom of a toilet bowl… stripping naked, stepping into a shower and closing its curtain… Water streaming from an overhead showerhead… Appearance of a human shape, first as a shadowlike image as seen by the woman through the translucent shower curtain, then in silhouette… with a knife in an upheld hand… Frantic stabbing in rapid-fire skipped frames… the victim against a white tile shower wall, slowly sinking… pulling down the curtain… Bloody water pouring into a round drain… and finally, the victim's lifeless round iris and dilated pupil juxtaposed with the round "weeping" showerhead.

When later asked why he made the movie, Hitchcock reportedly replied that "the murder in the bathtub, coming out of the blue, that was about all."

Filming the iconic scene had required seventy-eight camera set-ups and fifty-two cuts during twenty-six takes during an entire week—almost a third of the entire film's shooting schedule—and yet the actual killing, lasting only forty-five seconds, brilliantly captured the immediacy of the moment. In that regard—as well as its obvious voyeuristic quality—the scene was much like reality tv. The fakery, such as the use of casaba melons and beefsteak for stabbing sound effects was okay, but use of diluted chocolate syrup to represent draining blood…

At the end of the day, that kind of detail—passable because Hitchcock reportedly thought the black-and-white film would have been too "repulsive" in color—typified why watching movies as opposed to reality tv—*Psycho* as opposed to an episode of, say, *The Anna Nicole Smith Show*—required tedious suspension of disbelief.

Some kill their love when they are young/ Some when they are old/ Some strangle with hands of Lust/ And some with hands of Gold…

Passing by the almost waterless swimming pool in the Fountainblue Motel's open courtyard ten minutes later, a deflated inner-tube semi-floating in a shallow puddle of water brought to mind another classic film, and another character Larry identified with: the fictional screenwriter, Joe Gillis, as the poor sap appeared at the beginning of *Sunset Boulevard*… floating face down in a Hollywood swimming pool… dead by gunshots fired by the female lead. Among other gems in Gillis' posthumous monologue was the astute observation that audiences didn't know that somebody sat down and wrote a movie; they thought actors made it up as they went along.

Gillis had catered to the whims of Norma Desmond, a faded screen star not unlike Dorothy Drew a/k/a "Alice Liddell"… initially as the hired "doctor" for her own hopelessly bad script for a comeback movie based on the Salome-and-John the Baptist storyline… feeding her delusions of grandeur with the aid of her former husband and director… The ex reduced to a fawning butler, not unlike Joe, her degraded gigolo… unable to leave the lap of luxury, partly due to the the pathetic woman's threat to

kill herself… breaking up with his younger—not unlike Jill Wadsworth—love interest… and finally…

Almost fifty years after the movie's release, its script was adapted almost word-for-word for the Broadway musical stage. In the final scene… *And as dawn breaks over the murder house, Norma Desmond, famed star of yesteryear, is in a state of complete mental shock,* says a tv news reporter…

♫*Madame, the cameras have arrived*♫ her faithful butler sings. ♫*Lights! Cameras! Action!* ♫

♫*This time I'm staying/ I'm staying for good*♫ Norma sings. ♫*I'll be back where I was born to be/ With one look I'll be me*♫

Damnit, typically but no less infuriating, the copy-cat stage production won Tony Awards for Best Musical, Best Original Score, Best Book of a Musical, Best Actress, Best Featured Actor, Best This-and-That, without mention of the screenwriters who created the movie's plot, its characters, and the dialogue of the closely followed original story.

For each man kills the thing he loves/ By all let this be heard…

Approaching the Ps-'n'-Qs pool hall-'n'-cafe where the *RSOOK* cast and crew would be awaiting his direction, Larry noticed an odd-looking man standing among a crowd of sidewalk gawkers, with an ax on his shoulder.

The coward does it with a kiss/ The brave man with a sword…

Crimson Orgy, the now celebrated "cult" film written and directed by Sheldon Meyer came back to mind, specifically its famous final scene that mercifully, in a sense, brought to an end a series of plot developments and antics of villainous backwoods characters as unrealistic and unmemorable as those in the later so-called "splatter film", *Texas Chainsaw Massacre:*

Set in an abandoned sawmill in a remote area outside a small Florida town not unlike Henryetta, Oklahoma… *Crimson Orgy's* female star, "Barbara"—a clueless performer not unlike Alice Liddell, but younger and not unlike Jill Wadsworth—being assaulted by a serial killer, "Ace Spade"… in the background, the whirring of an old buzzsaw, identified in faded paint on its wooden base as "The Dismemberer".

Critics still disagreed about whether the ensuing melee involving multiple cast members—and possibly Sheldon Meyer—was scripted, or a spontaneous on-set incident that happened to be captured on film. The latter interpretation was supported by the set-up shot of Barbara's face, suggesting that it would have been tritely splattered with Ace Spade's blood-and-guts when she pushed her attacker into the teeth of The Dismemberer. Instead, however, she had joined the fray, and…

Larry grudgingly gave Sheldon Meyer credit for one masterstroke of reality filmmaking at the end: capture of the high keening sound of a perfect cathartic scream.

"Get a chainsaw," he facetiously advised the ax man as he entered the pool hall-'n'-cafe.

"Where in hell have you been?!" Dorothy Drew a/k/a Alice shouted. "This… this fake socialite refuses to speak her assigned lines. If not… fixed, and 'when done, done quickly', the season will go down the toilet like a…"

"Damnit, Larry, I scratched on your door 'til almost dawn!" Jill complained. "I've come up with the perfect season ending."

"I really must protest," Alice's usually mild-mannered personal assistant, Bruce, added. "The build-up of on-set tension has become intolerable, and dangerous for Alice."

"And in case you missed the memo," said a heavyset newcomer, ridiculously costumed in an old-fashioned, double-breasted suit, two-tone brown-and-white wingtips, and a felt fedora. "No way is Yours Truly Ms. Liddell's bodyguard or main squeeze, which should be made crystal clear to potential stalkers and Stans."

Ignoring the hubbub around him…

"Marty and the film crew will spend the remaining daylight hours on establishing shots to capture context," Larry announced.

And though he was yet to script an episode ending…

"We'll shoot the finale tonight at a location to be announced."

Retreating from clamor back toward his room, on impulse he leaned into the Best Boy's ear…

"Find a sawmill," he whispered, to his young protege. "And dig up a recording of that old song about reality tv by Lily Allen

that goes: ♫Forget about guns and forget ammunition/ 'Cause I'm killing them all on my own little mission♫ Got it?"

"Got it, Boss: The Big Enchilada, with extra catsup. Right?"

CHAPTER THIRTEEN

As expected of him in his role as Alice's longtime personal assistant, Bruce Von Mewling placed a tray on the motel room vanity where the *RHOOK* star sat, gazing into a mirror. He dutifully poured a cup of tea for her. Knowing she preferred that he not speak until spoken to, he bit his tongue.

Since announcement of the location for the shooting of the *RSOOK* season's final scenes, he'd been uneasy. Haunted by images from the *Texas Chainsaw Massacre* movie dating back to his childhood—even more so by the *American McGee Alice* video game in which the Dormouse and March Hare were depicted as tied to a monstrous dissection table—he thought of Larry Davis' selection of a nearby sawmill for tonight's filming as somehow ominous.

"The crumpets are stale," said his own Alice. "How many times must I tell you…"

"I strongly advise that you not continue to appear in the season finale," he blurted. "Larry's under a lot of stress. He's been acting stranger than usual. As put by Lewis Carroll to warn his Alice: 'Beware the Jabberwock! The jaws that bite, the claws that snatch/ Beware the Jubjub bird, and shun the fruminous bandersnatch!…'"

"Fiddle-de-dee. I have talked to Larry, and…"

"'He took his vorpal sword in hand…'"

"Nonsense. I am no longer concerned about adverse effect upon me of any untoward 'incident' Larry might stage. To the contrary, in fact, I rather expect a gripping lead-in to next season in which my star shall twinkle even brighter without, uh, dimming distractions."

Bruce didn't have the heart, nor stomach to go into the grisly details of the show's more likely, almost certain demise. Instead…

"Not to worry, Alice," he said. "I have been working on a next chapter of your career: *High Tea with Alice 2.0*, a daily podcast from my—or dare I say—our apartment, starring only you."

"Podcast?! Me, Alice Liddell, on a laptop, on a phone?"

"Podcasts are the new thing," he pointed out. "Influencers are the new celebrities. And your unedited advice on ladylike etiquette is more needed today than ever."

"I am a star, not a common 'influence peddler', and much too big for a small screen. Really, Dormy, you forget your place."

Stung by her haughty dismissal, made all the more hurtful by use of the demeaning nickname she had assigned to him almost twenty years ago—that of the lowly Dormouse used by Lewis Carroll's fictional Alice as a foot cushion—Bruce again bit his lip.

Damnit, he had discovered Dorothy Drew, a frivolous young would-be socialite versed only in mindlessly memorized rules of etiquette. He had launched her career on *High Tea* with a mass mail-out of personalized "Alice Liddell" notes to other members of the Oklahoma Junior League, who had dutifully responded with an initial batch of "fan mail". He had made the nobody into the avatar that then became a reality tv celebrity. And oddly despite her ridiculous affectations—though he could have carried on with his own tv career, and marriage—he had become perversely attached to "Alice Liddell".

Like a barnacle attached to a whale, as she might put it, he had remained at her side… or as he himself would put it, like the mouse who rescued Lewis Carroll's little "Alice" from the pool of her own tears, prompting her to ingenuously ask: "Who am I? Ah, that is the great puzzle."

No, in keeping with her public image, she had "outgrown" him, she would more genteelly put it. And that would be true in a way. She was now "big", grotesquely inflated by…

"As your 'Dormouse', such as were popular pets in Victorian England, I've not dared to prick your delusions, 'my dear'," Bruce now dared to say. "But now I must confess that for the

past nineteen years I myself have been the most devoted, and recently, virtually the only author of your adoring fan mail. Otherwise, most of what now comes in is snarky ridicule, along with outright hate for the real Alice Liddell: a maladjusted, self-absorbed, vulgar — yes, vulgar — two-bit would-be actress, adept only at glossing banality with tastelessly glamorized celebrity for the voyeuristic entertainment of equally vapid women and the amusement of misogynistic males."

"How dare you speak to me in such mannerless manner!"

"Consider it a final act of attentiveness, my dear. The woods around you are full of crazed stalkers such as the ones who have threatened and carried out vicious attacks against other celebrities. And a particularly menacing 'fan' who has seen the real person you are — having been inflamed by 'your' especially 'fond' notes to him and a lock of your wig enclosed with one — happens to reside in this godforsaken area."

"You have dared to correspond in my name with that rodeo clown?!"

"Oh no, I'm quite sure neither your ex-husband nor your abandoned daughter would want to have anything to do with you. Your locally-based fan — currently enraged no doubt to have not received an item of your underwear, as requested — is a man by the name…"

"Out!" she screeched. "You… you… you intolerably annoying dormouse!"

As Bruce turned to take his leave, words from *Wonderland* came to mind: *You've no right to grow older, the Dormouse said to Alice,* who was seven at the time.

As he closed the door behind him, later words from *Looking Glass* caught up to him: *Seven years and six Months! Humpty Dumpty repeated thoughtfully. Now if you'd asked my advice, I'd have said 'Leave off at seven.'*

Echoing inside his head as he walked along the edge of the motel's dilapidated pool: *One can't help growing older, said Alice.* **One** *can't, perhaps, said Humpty Dumpty, but* **two** *can. With proper assistance, you might have left off at seven.*

Hmmm, Bruce hmmed, as he entered his room, imagining a final *Real Socialites of Oklahoma* scene as Lewis Carroll—or he himself—might stage it for an overdue "Alice" swan song: *One, two! One, two! And through and through/ The vorpal blade went snicker-snack!*

CHAPTER FOURTEEN

♪**Oh, goodbye, cruel world/ I'm off to join the circus/ Gotta find a way to hide my...** ♪

Due to loud hubbub inside the Ps-'n'-Qs pool hall and quaint cafe, Max couldn't hear what the weatherman on the tv screen behind the bar was saying. But according to a map and graphic a current thunderstorm was due to have passed through the area within the next thirty minutes.

"It'll be past midnight when we shoot," said the youngish guy who had sidled up next to him and introduced himself as Marty Somebody, *RSOOK*'s "Best Boy" in charge of logistical arrangements. "Technically it'll be Friday by the time we shoot the Martini scene. That's Tinseltown lingo for a wrap usually <u>followed</u> by party time."

♪**I'm off to join the circus/ Oh, Mister Barnum, save a place for me...** ♪

Yeah, the joint was jumping. Booze was flowing like bloody noses in a back alley brawl. Ms. Liddell and other cast and crew members — not including the tall baldheaded personal assistant the *RSOOK* star usually had at her side — but even the bleach-blonde real housewife, Jill Wadsworth, looked to be having a ball.

"So with less than twenty-four hours before airing, there'll be overtime for everyone," the Best Boy noted. "Except for you, Maxie. You might as well go home and wait for a casting call for next season."

Lowry had already told him that—because he was not yet a member of an American Federation of Television and Radio Artists— his earlier on-camera appearances would be scrapped

and he would not be put in a frame of this season's final scenes. Mom would be disappointed, but next season…

♫**Shoot me out of a cannon, I don't care/ Let the people point at me and stare/ I'll tell the world…** ♫

The recorded music stopped as the Davis dude ankled into the room.

"Listen up," said the lookalike *a la* Woody Allen writer/director. "The final scenes will be shot at a remote location. So everybody needs to board the limo and vans within the next ten minutes in order to be at the abandoned sawmill by twelve-fifteen, sharp."

"Abandoned sawmill?!" the Wadsworth skirt shrieked, looking like she had wet her undies

Others in attendance moaned with what sounded like dread, if not also damp drawers.

Davis explained that he had researched the matter, and that the only local color he'd been able to come up with for an interesting backdrop to the final scenes was a legend about the sawmill.

The tale he went on to summarize sounded semi-familiar, and…

"But… But… But that sounds like the *Geico* commercial," the blonde whined. "The scary one starring the Jason Voorhees lookalike wearing a hockey mask in *Friday the Thirteenth III*. Chris Higgins slammed an ax into his head, but in *Friday the Thirteenth IV*… "

Oh yeah, Max now vividly recalled the horrifying scene of four young adults in terrified flight, coming upon a possibly haunted house during a spooky night:

Let's hide in the attic, said one.

*No, in the basemen*t, said another.

Why can't we just get in the running car? a savvy one asked, but…

Are you crazy! said a smarty-pants, looking toward an equipment shed. *Let's hide behind those chainsaws.*

Smart, they agreed, as a mope holding a chainsaw lifted his

mask to reveal a puzzled look on his kisser.

"If you're appearing in a horror scene—which is what today's reality tv audience wants—you have to make dangerous choices," said Davis. "It's what you do if you hope to have people keep watching."

Hmmm.

Maybe due to an obvious lack of enthusiasm on the part of most cast and crew members, the show's writer/ director stood up on a chair and…

"Some so-called experts claim it's impossible to capture reality on film," he stated more loudly. "And in a limited sense, they're right. An image on a television screen is literally an image on a television screen, not, say, an actual glass of milk that can be drunk. They say the best we can achieve is something called verisimilitude: an appearance of the real or true that convincingly depicts a world that is congruent with an audience's expectations about what the world is like, and this too is right to an extent. Under bright light, milk—epitomizing pure whiteness—appears to be somewhat translucent and slightly bluish, requiring substitution with a mixture of white paint and a thinning solvent to be accurately depicted on film.

"But when it comes to capturing the reality of human drama that evokes a visceral cathartic reaction in an audience capable of purging the soul of repressed thoughts and emotions… Well, I say, let's prove the experts wrong. Let's go out to that sawmill tonight and break a leg!"

♫**Goodbye, cruel world, we're off to join the circus…** ♫ the liquored-up barroom audience sang, as Max noodled his next move.

On the one hand, he'd agreed to detect threats to Ms. Liddell only through today, up to midnight at the latest. The only identifiable suspects of involvement in a possible plot to eliminate the *RSOOK* star-- the client's ex-husband and the show's writer/ director—had been eliminated as potential plotters by the potential victim herself. The show had its own security personnel to protect against unidentified potential stalkers and Stans in

the woodwork. And without a union card, he himself would not be allowed to appear in the final scene. But…

♫Well, the joke's on me, I'm off to join the circus… ♫

On the other hand, in the event of an "incident" Yours Truly was in line to star next season in a whodunnit *Real Socialites of Oklahoma* sequel.

♫Oh, Mister Barnum, save a place for me/ I'm off to join the circus… ♫

FRIDAY

April 11. 2025

CHAPTER FIFTEEN

♫**I'll take my clothes off and it will be shameless/ 'Cause everyone knows that's how you get famous...** ♫

During a pause in the action following a trip-and-fall by one of the tittering-and-tipsy real socialites—the overweight one named Wanda—a beam of moonlight squeezed through a gap in scudding clouds and... Max noticed that Alice Liddells' baldheaded assistant had joined the party... and seemed to be creeping behind a stooped-over crew member carrying some kind of equipment toward a looming barn-like structure.

Inside the semi-lit abandoned sawmill, moaning wind rattled loose wood siding... pigeons or maybe bats fluttered overhead... cobwebs hung like partly torn gauze curtains, partially obscuring a spotlit...

"What's that?" said a real socialite in an alarmed tone of voice.

"Ohhhhh," another real socialite whimpered.

The teeth of a large round buzzsaw, partially rusted but with its edges looking recently sharpened, glinted in partial light.

"OMG!" said the bleach-blonde socialite named Jill, staring wide-eyed at... in crudely daubed fresh bright red paint on the saw's heavy wooden base: DISMEMBERER!

"Let's get this over with, Larry," said Alice Liddell. "I need to see a man about... I need to visit a powder room."

Whirrr...

The blade began to spin.

"Step closer," the high-pitched voice of the show's writer/director directed. "Get emotionally naked."

Whirrrrr...

"Stop!' another man's voice commanded.

"The show must go on!" said another.

Whirrrrrrrr…

Out of shadowy background a bald head flashed…

Whirrrrrrrrr….

… then the silhouette of the still-stooped figure, holding overhead an ax!

Whirrrrrrrrrrr…

In filmy *noir*… OMG! A terrified scream… followed by whine of the sawmill blade slowing to a series of dull, moist *thunk-thunk-thunks*. . . and, ugh, a gruesome mixture of gray matter and blackish blood splattered onto the camera's lens!

"I'm so glad you chickened out of your case," said Max's mom from beside him on the den sofa. "For you to have personally witnessed such realistic spillage of gore would have permanently ruined your appetite for scrambled eggs with catsup."

"Yeah, quite an incident," Max agreed. "And a perfect set-up for a whodunnit sequel next season. I'm not one to leap to conclusions, but for Yours Truly's money—dollar-to-a donut—the likely doer, not to mention the likely victim…"

Buzz. Buzz. Buzz.

He put his phone to an ear and…

"Uh huh… Uh huh… Uh huh."

He put down the phone, and as credits began to roll on the tv screen…

"What is it, Max? You've gone white as the old *Pillsbury* doughboy."

"That was Lowry, the *Real Socialites of Oklahoma* Best Boy. The show's been cancelled, so thumbs down to a sequel."

"But why, Max?"

With a sigh, Max reported that—according to Marty Lowry—the incident staged by Larry Davis wasn't realistic enough to suit a so-called focus group out in LaLa Land. But as credits continued to roll…

♫I am a weapon of mass consumption/ Not my fault, it's how I'm programmed to function… ♫

In
Memoriam
Larry Davis
An anti-hero at best, obsessed with ambition to be
recognized for creation of catharsis through
capture of reality on film, who proved to not have
the stomach for imitating life with art by stepping
on his own punchline in an attempt to rescue the
intended victim in a final scene that otherwise
might have earned kudos.
R.I.P.
♫I don't know what's right and what's real anymore/ And I
don't know how I'm meant to feel anymore/ And when do you
think it will all become clear… ♫
THE
END